A Tooth Fairy's Promise

A Tooth Fairy's Promise

Book 1 in the Osseous Series

Michael J Adams

Derelict Books

To my family: Thanks for putting up with me all these years

To the FBI agents reading my search results: Thanks for not taking any hasty actions

To all my beta readers out there: Thank you for all your feedback

ALSO BY MICHAEL J ADAMS

The Osseous Series
Prequel: Tooth & Nail
Book 1: A Tooth Fairy's Promise
Book 2: Exiles
Book 3: Insiders
Book 4: Vibrations
Book 5: Replacements
Book 6: Newhires

Plagiarism

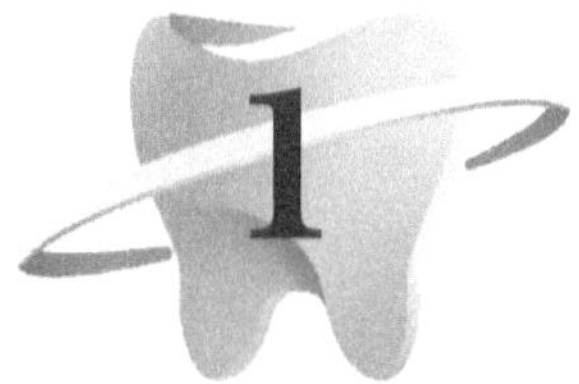

Squealing tires and the stench of burning rubber announced Tiffemory's arrival at Hartsfield-Jackson Atlanta International Airport. An airport parking employee in a high-vis green vest dove out of the way as her little Toyota hopped the curb. There was an awful crunch as the front of the car slammed into a concrete planter holding assorted ferns.

She wasn't driving under the influence but the tooth sitting in her belly was a distraction. Tiff slipped off her seatbelt and reminded herself why she usually had someone else drive her around while tracking down clients. If she was right about this lead, she didn't have time.

"What the hell are you doing?" the traffic attendant screamed as he got back to his feet and dusted off his hands. "You nearly took off my leg!"

Tiffemory pulled her keys from the ignition and grabbed the essentials from her bag. Her lone car key and her phone went into one of the back pockets of her jeans and her IDs into a small pocket on the sleeve of her red, V-neck blouse. A pair of bone-white chopsticks rested between her teeth.

The parking officer bounded forward and pounded his fist on the hood of her car. Tiff ignored him, stowed her purse under the seat, and sprinted toward the terminal.

He pointed at the yellow car that had seen better days. "You can't leave your car here," the man yelled after her.

The petite detective didn't slow her pace for anything. She twisted sideways, sneaking past a couple in Hawaiian shirts and sunglasses doing their best to block the pair of automatic doors into departures. As she ran, her eyes scanned heavenward for the appropriate airline. Finally, she spotted Southwest Airlines' rainbow-colored heart logo.

An old man in plaid pants and suspenders clogged up the walkway as he wandered along aimlessly. Instead of slowing, she leaped over the suitcase trailing behind him. She maintained her momentum and cut in front of the dozen and a half people in line. There was a dull thud as her body slammed into the ticketing counter.

"You've got to be shitting me. Hey, the line starts back there!" someone groaned from the middle of the line.

"I need some help, please," she mumbled through the sticks in her mouth. Nobody so much as glanced in her direction. Tiff slapped her drivers and private investigator licenses on the counter and yelled out. "It's an emergency."

A man in a crisp white shirt glanced over his shoulder in the middle of loading a massive suitcase onto the luggage conveyor. She tied her strawberry blonde hair into a sloppy bun and tucked the chopsticks away.

"You'll need to wait your turn in line, miss."

She swept her PI license from the counter and held it up for the representative to see. "I'm a private investigator and I need to get through security immediately. A child's well-being is at stake."

"I'm sorry, one moment," the Southwest Airlines agent said to an aggravated, balding businessman who had just stepped up to be served.

"I'm Dan, how can I help you?" the man said, picking up both of her ID cards. He looked down at the five-foot-tall woman for a long moment and then looked back at the cards. He started to hand them back and then repeated the process another four times.

Tiffemory tapped her fingers on the countertop. Just because she was used to the constant staring didn't make it any easier. And she knew rushing the man was only going to make him more suspicious. People's subconscious mind excelled at recognizing things that don't belong, even if it couldn't readily determine why.

"My client booked a flight on my behalf. I need my boarding pass printed ASAP." The fact that she had no intention of getting on the flight was irrelevant. She solely needed the ticket to get her past security and into the gate area.

Dan lifted the license one last time and compared the details against her appearance.

Tiff straightened her posture and smiled, hoping to portray a closer match to the photo. Her heart sped up. Both ID cards were fakes. They were high-quality forgeries—even the driver's license had her weight on the high side at one-twenty. Still, they were untested.

The man handed the cards back and took his sweet time henpecking her name into the keyboard.

Her stomach gurgled as a reminder time was short. It was going on seven hours now since she swallowed the child's tooth. It was nearing the end of the digestive cycle. Unfortunately, when the tooth broke down, so too would her bond to the child.

She closed her eyes and concentrated on the nagging sensation tugging her gut in his direction. The taut, intangible connection wanted to pull her toward the concourses. She focused on that connection. Time seemed to stop, and she lost all awareness around her as her consciousness propelled forward.

This was a method of sensing that Tiff hardly ever utilized. Aside from leaving herself vulnerable, it didn't reveal much. There was no way to judge distance or anything in the vicinity. Nevertheless, she saw the small, skeletal figure of her client's son—Bryce—shuffling forward in the darkness. He took a few steps and then came to a standstill before repeating the process a few more times.

More bad news. Not only was their connection close to snapping, but by the looks of his movement, he was in the process of boarding or already marching to his seat. She was screwed either way. Even if the bond held, there was no way of reaching the boy in time.

That left two options. The first was to exploit the connection between the two of them. Without much effort, she could command his bones in any number of ways that would make the takeoff stall due to a medical emergency. Unfortunately, that would be extremely unpleasant for him.

"No luggage today?" Dan asked. The question fell on deaf ears.

The other option was to run like hell and hope she reached him. Tiff snapped her eyes back open. Her brain struggled to fill in the images of the airport around her. She blinked several times to clear her vision and found the ticketing employee staring at her.

"I'm sorry..." she said.

"Luggage, Miss. I asked whether you had any."

Tiff shook her head. "No. I don't."

"Here's your boarding pass Miss Greenstone. Enjoy your flight."

The tooth fairy muttered her thanks, snatched the colored paper envelope and her IDs, and then took off into a sprint once again. She knocked over a pile of suitcases belonging to a family of four decked out in Disney gear. With more luck than grace, she managed to stay on her feet.

"Sorry," she mumbled without glancing back.

After elbowing and squeezing her way to the front of the security line, she arrived before an aging TSA agent with caterpillars for eyebrows. He glared at her through coke-bottle glasses. After a long moment, he held his hand up and pointed behind her.

"You're going to need to step to the back of the line and wait your turn."

Tiff held out her ID cards and ticket before leaning on his podium to catch her breath.

He stared at her hand until she removed it from his post. "Your flight isn't for another three hours," the agent said, glancing down at her ticket. "I'm going to need you to take your place at the back of the line."

"You don't understand, sir. I'm a private investigator and my client's child is in the concourse. His mother is about to violate her custody order by taking him over state lines. "

She bit the top of her lip and hoped she got that law right. There were so damn many of them.

"I haven't seen any recent AMBER alerts. What's the child's name and what gate are they at?" the agent asked skeptically, looking her up and down. "We'll have officers detain them at the gate."

Tiff shook her head quickly. If she knew that information, she'd gladly have told him. Unfortunately, all she had to go on was an unexplainable metaphysical connection.

"She has a history of violence and uniforms will only spook her. Please. You're wasting time that I don't have."

The agent looked deep into her eyes to cast judgment on her soul based on whatever he saw there. After a deep breath, he reached up for her papers and put them through their paces. It took longer than she liked.

Instead of fretting over whether her forged documents would trigger alarms, she ran back through the events of the day.

Somehow her information got passed along to Gregg—her current client. Naomi—Gregg's high school sweetheart and estranged wife—ditched rehab, trashed his house, and then ran off with their young son. It should have been an easy case, especially since six-year-old Bryce had lost his first tooth the night before. Unfortunately, she'd been delayed entrance to the house for several hours due to safety concerns. A paranoid officer mistook drywall dust for powdered Fentanyl.

Tiffemory dedicated several hours in the morning toward actual investigative work. There were several places Naomi could have taken the child. Besides her parents owning a house near Lake Redwine, Naomi was also a real estate agent. That meant a countless list of properties scattered around the city to search. While waiting for a hazmat team to clear the house and Gregg to dig the tooth from the trash, Naomi gained a sizable lead.

After wasting most of the day bouncing between rentals and overpriced homes, she finally felt the unmistakable pull of the boy near the airport. It was a risky move on Naomi's part, but Tiff should have expected it from a desperate mother.

Tiff shook her head. The one time she followed actual investigative procedures, and it bit her in the ass. Now she was at the mercy of a glorified airport security guard while the connection between her and Bryce frayed like a deteriorated steel cable.

After sweeping a handheld ultraviolet light across them he held them up to the camera built into the podium. The TSA agent finally scrawled an unidentifiable pair of initials on the ticket and handed the items back. "There aren't many precedents for this kind of thing."

"I understand. I'll yell for help if I need it."

Tiff skipped to the front of the scanner, threw her phone and keys into a tray, and took a calm step through the metal detector when someone waved her through. As soon as her items re-emerged, she pocketed them and took off down the hall. Her small frame darted around and between groups of people. As she turned a corner, she clipped a luggage carrier being pushed by a young man wearing a button-down shirt.

She tripped and fell face first. Instead of putting her arms out to brace herself, she tucked into a roll.

"I didn't see you, are you okay?" The porter said as he reached down to help her up. The man watched her take off again, shrugged his shoulders, and went about his way.

Tiff bolted through concourse C, relying on the gentle tugs from Bryce's bond to guide the way. Newsstands, luggage shops, and fast-food outlets blurred at the edge of her periphery. She ran on autopilot—letting muscle memory and raw sensory input to navigate a path—while allowing her other senses to probe the end of their shared tether.

Bryce was still out of visual range, but only a few gates away. And then the connection snapped.

The fairy kept running in the same direction. The boy was close. She knew it.

She called upon her other senses once again. All color leached out of the concourse and the hundreds of travelers scattered throughout it. One after another, an outline of a skeleton began to overlay each individual. They were fuzzy for a fraction of a second before coming into crisp focus. If she cared to, and there was enough time, she'd have been able to count each of the individual 206 bones.

Tiff slowed her pace. Somewhere among that skeletal army was Bryce; a single red ball, hidden beneath hundreds of shifting cups. She stumbled about in a slow circle. Her head began to pound. Trying to process the bones of people within her line of sight as well as those that glowed faintly through walls was a taxing endeavor. But the boy's unique skeletal structure was still imprinted on her mind. And she refused to give up.

She stumbled into a businessman who spilled his coffee. Ignoring his queries as to whether she was drunk, she kept moving in the direction she'd been heading. Gate C53 was all but empty. She rushed to the floor to ceiling windows. A massive Boeing 747 taxied along the runway.

Fifteen children were on the flight. Tiffemory didn't bother counting the adults. There, at the back of the plane, was Bryce. She was sure of it. But there was nothing she could do about it at this point.

Something tugged at her—first in her chest, and an instant later, over her entire body. It was more disturbing than painful, like how your skin sticks to your clothes when you pull it away on a muggy summer night. But it was constant. And it was not a good sign.

Color returned to the world and Tiff reached out for support. She stumbled backward and by some stroke of luck, landed in a seat.

The flight attendant at the gate walked over, the frown lines around her brow growing deeper.

"Are you okay?"

"I'm fine," Tiff said, a slight rasp in her voice.

She didn't realize until now how much she'd expended herself recently. The anchor keeping her in Atlanta was breaking down. If it failed like the bond to Bryce, she'd be banished back to the reality she came from. And if that happened before she reported back on the boy, he'd be lost too.

Tiffemory pointed out the window. "The flight that just took off. Could you tell me where it was headed?"

"Flight 1576 is going to Dallas Fort Worth. Are you going to need to reschedule?"

"No. I'm good. Thanks."

Tiffemory rested in the chair for a moment before backtracking through the concourse. She stopped when she found one of the large monitors tracking every flight going in and out of the airport. Halfway down the board, she found American Airlines flight 1576. In two and a half hours it would land in Texas.

She walked to the windows at the empty gate behind her and watched as other planes lined up across the various runways. She dug the cell phone from her back pocket.

"Gregg. Uh, Mr. Winters, it's Tiffemory Greenstone."

"Did you find my son?" There was a faint stagger in the man's voice.

She took a deep breath and chewed at a patch of raw skin on her upper lip. Luckily, she didn't often have to relay bad news.

"I'm afraid that I wasn't able to get to the airport on time. Naomi and Bryce boarded the plane. However, you can let the authorities know that they're on American Flight 1576. It lands at Dallas Fort Worth at 7:30 local time."

To her surprise, Gregg didn't yell. He didn't inquire as to why she didn't call the police as soon as she realized his wife and son were at the airport. There was a heavy sigh of relief.

"I don't know how you managed to track him down before the police had a clue but thank you."

The relief didn't just show in his voice. Tiff's cheeks warmed. Her pulse quickened and could be felt down in her toes.

Tiffemory barely understood how the whole thing worked. Whatever powerful unknown forces in the universe that governed physics—and whatever else—also kept Outsiders in check. She didn't know if it worked this way across the board, but for her to remain in Atlanta, she had to ingratiate herself to the people who belonged here.

Even though she hadn't delivered Gregg's son to him, her actions strengthened her anchor enough to keep those forces at bay. The creepy sensation pulling at the very fabric of her being ceased immediately.

"You don't know what this means to me."

"Glad to help. And I'm not using the ticket you booked for me. If you cancel it, you should be able to get a credit."

"Thank you again, Tiff. I'll slip the payment under your office door as you requested."

Tiff ended the call, smiled, and followed the signs overhead back toward the ticketing booths.

Tiffemory hugged the corner and left the wing containing the C gates and headed back into the main concourse. At the same time, an obese bald man took the turn sharply. His eyes were cast downward, focused upon the young girl he pushed in the wheelchair. Tiff had to sidestep to prevent her foot from being run over.

She pivoted on the balls of her feet preparing to give the man a mouthful but hesitated. It was difficult to be too angry when she'd done the same to the parking attendant earlier. As she turned to go, she did a double-take. Something nagged her about the man that she couldn't place. For whatever reason, the folds of fat on the back of his neck looked familiar.

After giving some time for other travelers to fill the void between them, she veered to the far-right side of the walkway and tailed the man. Judging by the well-tailored suit, it was obvious he wasn't a porter. Although he walked without urgency, he didn't yield at all to anyone, almost running over a handful of other people. The longer she followed him, the more she was sure it was paranoia. It was ridiculous to think she recognized someone by the girth of their neck. But she had nowhere else to be.

To put her mind at ease, she quickened her pace and closed the gap. When she got ahead of the man, she knew she had seen him before. His features were familiar. However, she couldn't place why.

Tiff stuck near the opposite end of the corridor and shifted her scrutiny to the figure in the wheelchair. The girl, probably in her mid-teens, slept peacefully with her head resting against a small pillow. The first thing that stood out was her hair. It was cut short and uneven and dyed a dirty blonde that didn't even cover her brown roots.

In her experience—provided the girl and her stylist were both sober—a teenage girl would sooner die than leave the house looking like this. Especially when she was in such an eye-catching emerald dress. Her eyes moved to her feet next. A stark white plaster cast stretched from her bare left ankle and disappeared somewhere beneath the dress. The cheap pair of sandals hanging off her feet clashed with the rest of her outfit.

Tiff directed her gaze to the cast and let her eyes shift out of focus. Her senses reached out and poked and prodded at the bones standing out in stark contrast. Tiffemory poked and prodded at the Femur, the largest bone and strongest bone in the body. There were no signs of fractures or breaks—either current or past. She inspected the Tibia, Fibula, and Patella in turn.

The bones were all in perfect health. There were a number of muscles and ligaments somewhere in between that she hadn't yet committed to memory. While her powers didn't afford her the ability to investigate any of them, it seemed unlikely. There was no reason for this girl to be in a cast.

There were too many things that didn't add up.

When Tiff shifted her investigation to the man pushing the wheelchair, she recognized him immediately. It was hard not to based on his bone structure. A natural honeycomb pattern at the cellular level gave bones their lightness and strength. His bone structure was weakened from osteoporosis. While not necessarily an uncommon thing for lifelong smokers or the elderly, this had a different cause. The irregular deformations and jagged edges like branch coral was a definitive sign of bone cancer.

Her eyes shift back into focus just in time to dodge around a pillar in her path. She'd never learned the man's name—just that he was somehow involved with a human trafficking ring. The question more important than his identity was why the man wasn't in prison.

He was one of three men involved in the Mallory Sanderson kidnapping roughly six months ago. While all her cases were memorable, hers was unforgettable. Before getting involved in the case, Tiff had no idea the ringleader was another fairy. She considered herself lucky to get out alive.

The kidnapper pushed the wheelchair to the back row of seats at a gate and took a seat. During their first encounter, she sucker-punched the huge man. She had no qualms about doing it again.

Tiff snuck up from behind and let her hand hover near his back. She reached out with her power, hoping Bryce's father had given her enough to spare. His bones shone through his back. Within a few seconds, Tiff followed the bumpy curve of his spine. She identified the precise locations where his second through fifth ribs connected to the vertebrae and around to the sternum. Holding onto that image, she swept around to the front of the aisle.

She bent over and wrapped the man in a hug. He gasped, recognizing her immediately. That was the precise moment when she took hold of his bones. Bits of her power seeped outward through their invisible connection and willed his bones into submission.

Before he could do anything, his ribs contracted, tightening like a snare around a wild hare. They forced the breath from his lungs and simultaneously prevented them from refilling. His hands went to his chest as he failed to draw breath.

"I warned you last time," she whispered. "This is strike two."

Wasting no time, Tiffemory patted down his pockets and palmed his wallet. She stood, took a step aside, and walked off with the wheelchair.

"Someone help!" She yelled. "I think this man's having a heart attack."

The gate came alive with people rushing to action. Tiffemory looked up at the digital clock in the terminal and noted the time. Supposedly, the brain could go about six minutes without oxygen before irreversible brain damage. She wasn't keen on killing people—even if they technically deserved it. She was a guest in Atlanta and felt abided to play by the rules... Most of them anyway. It was comforting enough knowing he'd have a bruise on his chest only rivaled by a kick from a mule.

A pair of paramedics raced past as she rolled the young girl past the security checkpoint and back into the main entryway. There, she pulled the wheelchair into the handicapped stall of the women's bathroom. She flipped open the brown leather wallet. An unsecured Georgia driver's license fell face down on the tiled floor. She picked it up and turned it over.

The picture on the ID was for Grace Davis and the picture matched the girl now in her care. She didn't know much about fake IDs, but she looked it over anyway. All the personal information seemed appropriate, and it was even signed in a flowery woman's script.

One thing that seemed out of place was the fact that the expiration date was two years from now. It seemed off because the card showed neither signs of discoloration nor the wear expected from a three-year-old license. It also seemed a little suspicious that the girl was wearing the same dress as in the photo. She was fairly certain the ID was a forgery. She made a mental note to reach out to her contact later for confirmation.

Tiff pulled the chopsticks from her hair and planted a small kiss upon it. She let her breath out through her nose and envisioned a simple cup. The pieces of bone shifted and became fluid in her hands. They flattened together to a disc before the edges rose to match her specifications. She filled the small cup with water from the sink and splashed it onto the girl's face.

"Wake up, honey," she said adding a few playful slaps against her face.

Grace's eyes flickered a little and fought to open fully. Her fingers flexed, trying to regain feeling. The girl's movements were sluggish as she desperately tried to determine where she was.

"I think you've been given a tranquilizer. There's not much we can do about that until it wears off. But you'll be okay. My name's Tiff and you're safe for now."

Tiff turned her head to the side and let out a low hiss. This wasn't the first drugged kidnapping victim she'd seen, but it was the first in a fake cast. Whoever was behind the group was getting smarter. So far, she hadn't found any leads on the individuals responsible.

The girl took a while stirring and raised a hand to wipe her eyes.

"It's okay. Take your time, Grace."

"What?" the girl mumbled.

"Your name isn't, Grace, is it?"

The teenager shook her head slowly and licked her lips before responding. "No. It's Dawn. What's going on?"

"Do you live in Atlanta?

Dawn nodded and Tiff gave a little sigh of relief. At least she was near home.

"You're at the airport. Did you have plans to visit friends or something, Dawn?"

"No."

"I didn't think so. Okay. Let's get you home. But first things first, let's get you out of this cast."

The girl's eyes fixated on the cast. "But my leg..."

"Trust me. It isn't broken."

Tiff pulled out her phone and did a quick calculation. Five minutes. She probably needed to address Dawn's captor. Tiff closed her eyes and focused inward. A silvery connection somewhat similar, but weaker than the one she shared with Bryce, came into view. She severed it from her end and allowed the man's ribs to move back to their correct anatomical positions.

Her Leatherman multitool was in the car—it never would have made it through security—so she made do with what she had. Tiff held the cup out of the girl's view and focused. Once more the bone became malleable beneath her fingertips. It elongated into a hook-shaped stick before the entire curve tapered off to a razor-sharp edge. Tiff knelt beside Dawn with the tool and wedged it between her thigh and the top of the cast.

"Try to sit still, hon. I'll have you out of there in a few minutes," Tiff said before beginning to pull it through the hardened plaster. Dawn was still groggy and didn't inquire about the cutting implement.

As much as she hated to, she had to give the scumbags credit for their ingenuity. Drugging a victim and casting their leg not only took away their mobility without causing any actual harm, but it also lent credibility to the wheelchair.

In a few minutes, the cast was cut from end to end. Tiff returned the tool to a pair of innocuous-looking chopsticks and stashed them back in her bun. Together, she and Dawn pried the plaster apart and freed her leg.

"Thank you," Dawn said with a sigh of relief. She braced herself and lifted her butt from the chair, but Tiff pressed down on her shoulder.

"Relax. I'll push."

Dawn dropped her bottom back down in the chair. As she did, something in the cargo web beneath rattled. Tiffemory bent down, picked up Dawn's purse, and handed it to her. The girl immediately opened it and dug around.

"My glasses are gone. The same goes for my phone."

Tiff pulled open the door to the stall and pushed her out. "They're replaceable. You're not."

Once outside, Dawn rubbed her hands along her bare shoulders for warmth in the chilly evening air. Tiffemory wished she had a jacket to give the girl, or better yet, had taken her captor's jacket.

A surge of heat cascaded through Tiff's body. Her toes curled in her sneakers and her entire body tingled. She felt as though fire would have poured forth from her mouth if her jaws weren't tensed. The wheelchair came to a halt as she closed her eyes and savored the feeling.

It would have lasted longer if not for the backfire of a passing truck. Tiff's eyes came open and settled upon the tow truck moving into position in front of her vehicle. She hurried to the curb and helped Dawn from the chair into the front seat.

The parking officer ran up to her, waving his arms as she slammed the passenger door shut.

"Get her out of the car, it's being towed. The police are on their way to ticket you for reckless driving and destruction of property."

The tow truck driver, a skinny man in a mesh hat and tan coveralls, stepped out. His eyes swiveled between Tiff and the angry security guard and then over to the empty wheelchair.

"Yeah... I'm not getting involved in this," the driver said before turning around and heading back to his truck.

"She's in a tow zone," the man shouted, running toward the tow truck. "Tow the car!"

Tiff left the wheelchair at the curb, jumped into the car, and merged back into traffic. She gunned the engine too soon before letting off the brake, leaving another set of smoking tire marks behind for the heartless attendant. Dawn turned around and cracked a smile as the man shook his fists.

After turning up the heat, Tiff glanced over at the young girl fighting to keep her eyes open. Dawn jumped slightly as Tiff patted her knee.

"Are you okay? The people who took you didn't hurt you, did they?"

"No," Dawn said, shaking her head. "I... Thanks for getting me out of there, Tiff. How the hell did you find me? I didn't know anyone was looking for me."

"I'm a private investigator and happened to be at the airport working on another missing person's case. The man who was trying to put you on a flight out of here and I have had a prior run-in. When I saw you with him, I knew something wasn't right. I'm pretty good at finding people, though I'll admit running into you was a happy little accident.

"We can discuss this further, but maybe you want to give me some directions first. I'm not as good at stumbling upon people's houses as I am people."

Dawn turned to stare out the window.

"It doesn't matter. I can't go home."

Tiff sat up straighter. Her fingernails dug into the steering wheel and the taste of copper filled her mouth as her teeth drew blood from her upper lip. She didn't want to ask but had to.

"Abuse?"

Dawn gave a single shallow nod.

"Your stereotypical asshole stepfather situation. But it's not like *that*. I mean he doesn't hit me or touch me."

"Mental abuse can cause just as much harm. I'd be glad to come inside and confront him with you." Tiff licked her lips and turned to look at her passenger. "I've had good luck with making sure these kinds of things don't continue to happen."

Dawn sniffled and cracked a smile. The smile slowly turned down as she turned and studied the fairy's face.

"Why do I believe you?"

Tiff smiled and returned her eyes to the road.

"There are alternatives if you can't go home. Atlanta has over a dozen different women's shelters around the city. I know the staff at a few of them personally. We could go there until you figure out a permanent arrangement."

"I stayed with my boyfriend's family for a couple of weeks. They knew I was having a rough time at home. But I started to feel like a burden, so I told them I'd smoothed things out.

"I picked up as many extra waitressing shifts as possible to keep me away from home. I got to talking about family stuff with one of the guys in the kitchen after hours who told me about an opportunity. He'd been living out of his car but moved into a temporary boarding house he heard about. I figured it was worth checking out.

"The boarding house turned out to be an abandoned motel on the outskirts of the city. It seemed kind of sketchy, but there were plenty of private rooms to go around. Granted, said rooms were empty save for a cot and a few cheap blankets, but it was supposedly temporary while they acquired more funding. The place had warm water, no rules, and trays of catered food brought in for breakfast.

"After being there a couple of days, a counselor made rounds for job placement opportunities. They handed out interview clothes, took headshots, and even held a workshop to assist with résumé writing. Despite telling them that I already had a job and still had another year of high school to finish, they insisted. I guess that should have been a red flag."

"You can't blame yourself. This sounds like part of an organized ring with deep pockets. What happened next?"

"That same night I awoke with an awful burning pain in my left leg. I dragged myself off the cot and tried to get help. I didn't make it far before collapsing. The same staff member who showed me around on my first day was already coming my way. I found that weird because the staff usually disappeared at night. He told me an ambulance was on the way and helped me back into the room.

"A paramedic arrived shortly after. He gave me a bottle of water, gave me a quick check, and then attached a splint to my leg. He said it was either a sprain or a fracture and that we'd have to go to the hospital for X-rays and further treatment. But that didn't make any sense. How do you break a leg sleeping?"

"You don't," Tiff said, though it came out as more of a low growl. "Did you hear any sirens or see the flashing lights of the ambulance?"

"No," Dawn said sheepishly.

"How many medics were there?"

"Only the one." Dawn let her head hang. "And now that I think about it, the man already had the splint in hand. I should have known something was fishy."

Tiff ground her teeth. This started to sound more and more like part of a larger plan set in motion long ago. It reeked of Jeck. Who better to orchestrate phantom broken legs than her favorite rogue tooth fairy?

"I'll need the name of the restaurant you worked at as well as the location of the motel."

"Of course. If it will help you stop them."

"The more I have to go off, the more likely that becomes. Now, how about I take you back to your boyfriend's house. We can explain everything to them and call the police."

Dawn nodded.

Tiff leaned forward and grabbed her purse from beneath the seat. She placed it on the center console.

"Can you grab my phone and plug your boyfriend's address into the navigation? Also, there's a spiral-bound notebook in my purse. Would you mind jotting down the address and whatever other pertinent information you can recall? I probably should have been recording our talk but I'm not great with technology."

Dawn found the phone and the notebook and left detailed notes.

Following the navigation prompts led them a few dozen miles in the opposite direction they'd been traveling. Tiff stopped asking questions and the girl seemed content to enjoy the silence and eventually drifted off.

Tiff pulled into the U-shaped drive in front of a two-story house with blue siding. A motion-activated light came on as she stopped near the front door. She reached over and gently shook her passenger awake.

"Sorry. I guess I dozed off." Dawn wiped a small bit of drool from her lip and opened the door. She lingered in the seat for a moment and glanced back at the wallet sitting beside Tiff's purse.

Tiff picked up the wallet and held it in her hands. "You don't want to know his name; it'll do nothing but haunt you. Trust me that I'll take care of this."

Dawn gradually raised her eyes from the wallet to the fairy's chubby face. "Yeah... You're probably right."

Tiff opened the wallet and surprisingly found a small wad of folded fifties and hundreds. She pulled them out and passed them over to Dawn.

"It doesn't make up for anything you've been through, but here. Better you have this than him. Use it to replace your glasses and phone—just make sure to get a new number."

The teenager stuffed the bills into her purse and then got back into the car before wrapping her arms around her savior.

"I can walk up with you if you like," Tiff said, returning the squeeze. "If you want some help explaining things."

"I'll be okay. Kevin's dad is huge and imposing, but he's a gentle giant. As long as I've known him, he's treated me like his own daughter. He'll understand."

Tiff thought about her own family and swallowed back the lump forming in her throat. "Cherish that, even if they're not your real family. You never know how long anyone has." The fairy coughed and did her best to keep a tear from forming in her eye.

"If you need anything. Anything at all, don't hesitate to call." Tiff pulled a slightly bent business card from a storage slot in the dash. "And the offer to set your stepdad straight still stands."

Dawn laughed and took the card.

"I left my number in your notebook and the address here too. If I can help in any other way, please let me know. I don't know how else to thank you..."

"Another hug will do," Tiffemory said with a smile. They shared another embrace. There was still a residual heat coming off the girl, but the fairy didn't get swept up in it this time. Either she'd absorbed all she could, or it was a one-time deal.

Tiff waited in the car until the front door opened. Dawn stood awkwardly at the threshold before a bear of a man that could only be Kevin's dad. There was a brief exchange before the figure embraced her. Dawn turned back and waved before disappearing into the house. Tiff waved back and shifted the car into drive.

Kevin's father—all six-foot-five and two hundred fifty muscular pounds of him—held up his hand signaling her to wait. She put the car in park and rolled her window down when the man stepped in front of the car and came around to her side.

When he dropped to one knee beside the car and still managed to maintain eye level with her, Tiff understood Dawn's giant comment. He had short, cropped hair, a broad nose, and a small spacer in each of his earlobes. However, what drew Tiff's attention most was the number of laugh lines around his clean-shaven face.

"Pleased to meet you. I'm Mitchell, Kevin's dad," he said, sticking one of his enormous mitts into the car.

"Tiff," she said and leaned back slightly so she had enough room to shake his hand.

The man's handshake was electric. She broke free from his grip as soon as she could. Her eyelids fluttered and she did her best to stick to the conversation.

"Dawn briefly told me what you did for her. I don't know how to repay you. Would you like to come in?"

"I appreciate the offer, but no. There are things I need to follow up on immediately to ensure nobody else gets hurt."

Mitchell nodded. "Then I won't hold you up any longer. Is there any way I can repay you in the future?"

Tiff shook her head. "It was my pleasure. Just take care of her."

"Rest assured that I will do just that." Mitchell bowed his head and smiled. "Thank you for everything you've done. Good luck finding these guys." The massive man returned to the house.

Tiff watched him walk away and somehow got the feeling he knew exactly what she was about to do. She pulled the car to the edge of the driveway and then flipped open the stolen wallet again. Charles Weston lived inside Atlanta proper and was an organ donor. So at least he had that going for him. As much as she wanted to pay the man another visit tonight, she'd put it off until tomorrow.

Her primary concern was alerting any other potential victims at the abandoned motel posing as a boarding house.

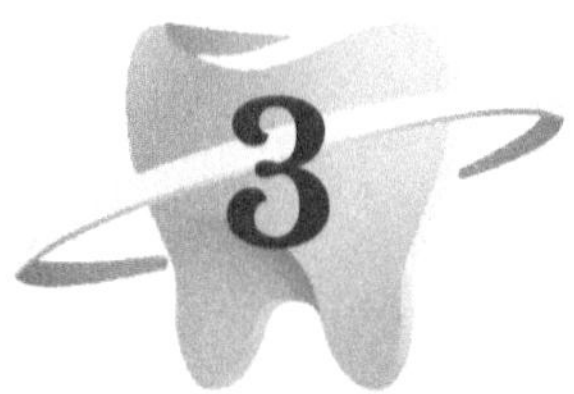

The Sunnyside Motel had been abandoned for at least a couple of years. The squat, blue and yellow brick building sat quiet and unlit, save for faint light sneaking around the curtains of a few rooms. While the exterior didn't qualify as dilapidated, it showed the usual signs of wear and tear and the abundant graffiti expected from an unused property. Tiffemory pulled into the pothole littered parking lot and killed the engine. She grabbed the dark black Leatherman multi-tool from her purse and locked the car up.

As she approached the pitch-black office, she realized the lights weren't just off. A dark film riddled with air bubbles coated the interior of the windows. Cupping her hands over her eyes, she peered inside. It was difficult to make out anything, but there were no signs of movement within.

Tiff plucked the chopsticks from her hair. They became putty in her hand and took on the rough shape of a key. She inserted it into the lock and forced the top edge of the shaft to undulate. The ridges rose and fell in tandem as she put gentle pressure on it. Each pin slid into position and the door swung open. Tiff looked over her shoulder and slipped inside. Her fingers groped along the wall until she located the light switches.

The fluorescent lights hummed and flickered to life. Half a dozen card tables lined the perimeter of the room, uncomfortable-looking metal folding chairs spaced evenly around them. Tiff walked the length of the room several times looking for any leads. The place was clean aside from the rectangular imprint of a laptop on the dusty countertop and a piece of clear tape on the wall with a torn corner of blue paper beneath it.

There was probably evidence here, but not for her. Forensic experts could easily pull prints off any of the tables or chairs, but it wasn't exactly evidence of anything other than trespassing. If the tape on the wall belonged to a banner or flyer for a fake charitable organization, it was long gone. If Tiff had to wager a guess, anything of import got packed up after Charles managed to draw a breath.

Tiff shut off the lights and locked up behind her. As she withdrew the key from the lock again it transformed back into the slender, bone-white sticks. She stashed them back into her hair and started going door-to-door. The first four rooms were dark and nobody answered her calls. A shirtless man with bits of mulch clinging to the bottom of his jeans appeared in the doorway of room five. The faint aroma of damp grass and cheap beer clung to him.

"Yeah?"

"Would you mind answering a few questions?"

The man, probably a few years older than Dawn, glanced past the fairy and out into the parking lot.

"I'm not a cop if that's what has you worried. My name is Tiff and I'm friends with Dawn. The tall blonde girl who stayed here for a few days. She disappeared last night. I was trying to piece together information."

The young man's hunched shoulders rclaxcd. Tiff lowered her head pensively and noted the details of the room behind him. Like Dawn mentioned, the room was mostly bare. There was no cot in sight, but she did notice the dark pink silhouette against the wall where a headboard rested some time ago. Empty beer cans littered the floor—though those were almost certainly from the room's current occupant.

"I'm not around much during the day and I keep to myself otherwise. Sorry I couldn't help."

Tiff frowned. "Do you know if there are any vacancies?"

He shrugged. "Probably. You'll have to come around early in the morning. There's usually someone around in the office in the morning. Especially on Monday to collect the week's rent."

Tiff's ears perked up. Dawn hadn't said anything about rent. She made it sound like the place operated as a shelter.

"How long have you been here?"

"The last three weeks or so."

"Ever see anything strange?"

"Strange? Other than the fact that this operation is off the books? No. This place is better than living on the street." The man scratched the side of his nose. "Do you need anything else? The rest of my six-pack is getting warm."

When Tiff paused for a moment, he began to shut the door.

"I have one last question." She gestured to the beer cans. "Did the people in charge hook you up with a fake ID?"

"What? No. It's not hard to find a place that sells to minors."

"Did they offer to take your picture?"

"Yeah... I've seen them do that on occasion. I felt it was a waste of time. And it was purely voluntary."

"Alright. Thanks for your time. A word of wisdom... This place may not be as safe as it appears."

He shrugged and then pulled the door closed. Before she could walk away it opened again to a slit. "Hey," he said. "I hope you find your missing friend."

Tiff nodded her thanks and stepped away from the threshold. There were other rooms with lights in the windows. Though it was likely a waste of time trying to get information out of anyone there.

Instead, she walked around to the front of the building, sweeping over the building with her other senses. She took cautious steps to ensure she didn't trip over a pothole or pile of rubbish. When she reached the end of the property she ducked around the corner and waited a moment for her vision to adjust back to normal. Three cars sat in the alley. All of them were older models speckled with rust.

She made her way back to her vehicle, counting the rooms as she went. The motel had six occupants spread among the twenty-four rooms. They all seemed relatively healthy, at least based on the structure of their bone health. And none of them shone brightly—the telltale sign of her kind.

Tiff climbed back behind the wheel, parked across the street, and stared out the window. This operation didn't spring up overnight. It was well planned. The other thing bothering her was that the building had been sitting empty for a while. The sudden activity should have drawn someone's attention. Either someone bought the building or was otherwise convincing authorities to stay away. Tiff made a mental note to investigate the records for the property.

Then there were the other inconsistencies. Dawn disappeared after a few days, but the kid she spoke to mentioned living there for weeks without incident. Either he wasn't what they were looking for... Or he wasn't what they were looking for right *now*. Tiff shuddered. The abandoned motel wasn't exactly the Marriott but attracted plenty of potential victims. On top of that, the rent generated went to fund more kidnappings.

Interrupting Dawn's kidnapping attempt would have the traffickers spooked, but it wasn't safe to let this place continue to operate. Tiff grabbed her phone and let out a long sigh. Alerting the police department would put these people back on the streets or in their cars. But at the same time, they were no safer here.

She stared out the window while punching 911 into her cell.

"I'd like to report a domestic disturbance. I took my dog for a walk and passed by the old Sunnyside Motel on Harriet Street. I thought the place was abandoned, but I heard shouting and saw a light on."

"We'll have a patrol car check it out," replied the dispatcher.

"Thanks."

Tiff watched the building until a pair of squad cars pulled into the parking lot. She kept an eye on the officers as they went from room to room and talked with each occupant. There were no altercations, and to her relief, no arrests. The young man she talked with walked to the back of the building, hopefully, to sleep in his car until he was sober enough to drive.

The authorities waited around until the other occupants either drove off or walked away. When all was quiet, Tiff fished Dawn's fake ID out of her purse and flipped it around in her fingers. It was only eight thirty. That left enough time to follow up on one more lead if she could reach her contact.

She searched through her phone and located Joshua's number. He was the first contact she'd made in Atlanta a little over a year ago. Her elders said he'd provide her with whatever she needed to get started with a new life. Joshua provided her with her driver's license and later the PI credentials. He was more than a simple hacker and counterfeiter, though. Tiff didn't know much about him other than the fact that he was part of a small network of people dedicated to helping others—including domestic abuse victims looking to start new lives.

Her call went directly to his voicemail.

Tiff scratched her head. Although they didn't speak on the regular, they occasionally pointed potential clients in each other's directions. And she'd never known him not to answer the phone. She dialed the number again.

"You've reached THM Designs. Unfortunately, we're no longer accepting new clients. Sorry for the inconvenience."

"Hi Joshua, it's Tiffemory," she said when she got his voicemail. "I have a project I was hoping to get a quote on. Please call me back."

Tiff hung up the phone and started the engine. As she shifted the car into drive, her phone rang. An unknown number.

"Hello?"

"Did you need some help?" Joshua's voice sounded preoccupied, if not pained.

"Yes. I was hoping we could meet in-person. I helped a girl out of a difficult situation this afternoon and need to run down some leads."

"Uhm... It's going to take me a bit. I'll see you where we first met in about thirty minutes."

Before she could reply, Joshua hung up. Tiff tossed the phone into her purse and headed to the dive bar on the opposite side of the city.

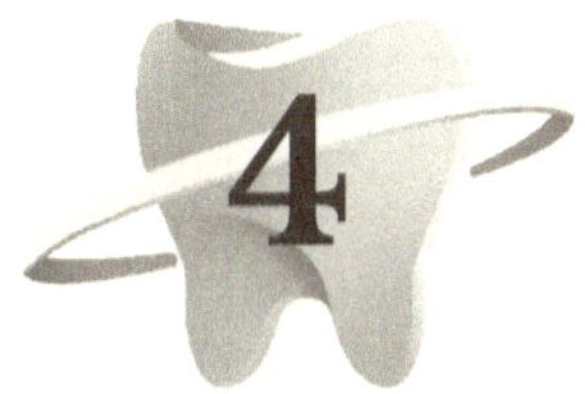

If The Derelict had a jukebox, it would have stopped the moment the blonde-haired fairy entered. She'd only been inside the bar once a year ago. It looked the same and she felt just as out of place. The interior bore a maritime shabby chic aesthetic. Hemp fishing nets sagged from the ceiling. Suspended inside them were plastic crabs, seagulls, and whatever else the locals threw in there—including an all too creepy sex doll. Rusted portholes dotted the walls above plaques detailing their ship of origin. The place was equal parts awe-inspiring and tetanus-inducing.

Half a dozen people crowded around a table at the back. A system pumping white noise through speakers in the ceiling reduced the sound of their shenanigans to a dull roar. Other than a few other people spread here or there drinking alone, most of the seats were empty.

A bartender almost as big as Mitchell followed Tiff with his eyes while chewing on a toothpick. He wore a light grey button-down work shirt with a silk-screened logo of a local brewery. His arms bore the muscles of a professional boxer and enough skull-oriented tattoos to pass as an ex-con.

Tiff trudged forward across the floor thick with discarded peanut shells and grabbed the nearest barstool. If the brass clock shaped like a ship's wheel was accurate, Joshua wouldn't show for another fifteen minutes. She took a minute to inspect the rusted anchor dangling precariously above the bar. How it hadn't fallen and killed the proprietor since her last visit was a mystery.

The bartender shook his head, letting out a snort through his nose, and then walked over.

"Are you sure you're in the right place?" he said, crossing his arms and leaning against the bar top. "I don't have the ingredients to whip you up a cosmopolitan, sweetheart."

"That's okay," the fairy said with a smile. She interlaced her fingers and added, "alcohol isn't really my thing."

The man snorted again and started to turn away.

"You've got grenadine," Tiff said, pointing to a shelf behind the bar. "How about a kiddie cocktail?"

"A kiddie cocktail..." The toothpick barely hung onto his upper lip as he repeated the request.

"Heavy on the syrup, please."

The man turned his back and begrudgingly mixed the fairy a drink.

"One kiddie cocktail for Shirley Temple." He slammed the glass on the concrete bar top, splashing the sugary drink everywhere. At the same time, a hollering erupted from the back of the bar.

Tiff set a five-dollar bill on the bartop. She took a sip of the blood-red drink and closed her eyes for a second to savor the sweetness before swiveling the stool in the direction of the commotion.

A handful of men cheered from beside a pool table covered in red felt. She craned her neck but saw no one playing billiards. The action was at a table beside it. Two men sat across from one another, their right arms clasped together and their elbows resting in puddles of spilled beer. The one closest to her wore a stocking cap and a black Harley-Davidson tee. Opposite him sat a man in a sweat-stained wife-beater tee.

The crowd cheered as Harley slammed the other man's hand down to the table. He swiped up a pile of bills and shoved a plastic beer pitcher into the loser's chest.

Wife-Beater waddled out of his way to sidle up next to her. His seasoned beer belly rubbed against the bar as he handed the pitcher across.

"Fill it up again, Cary." The man sucked at something stuck in his teeth and casually turned his head in her direction. He smiled a large gap-toothed smile. "Is it ladies' night?"

Cary laughed and set the full pitcher back down. Wife-Beater hiked his pants up and wandered closer to the fairy, letting two fingers caress the edge of the counter.

"Our table could use a pretty little cheerleader." He leaned close enough for her to smell the stink of beer on his breath. "Why don't you join us?"

Tiff set down her drink. "I appreciate the invite, but I'm waiting for a friend. Besides, I'm not sure any of you guys could handle me."

Wife-beater chuckled and looked back at Cary who shot him a glance suggesting he behave himself.

"You've got quite the mouth on you. I can think of a few better uses for it."

Tiff pounded the rest of her drink and shrugged. Until Joshua showed up, she didn't have anything better to do. She hopped off the stool.

"Alright," she said, marching past him. "Let's go embarrass you in front of your friends."

She headed to the back of the bar, straddled the bench at the open end of the table, and cleared her throat. All four people gathered turned to stare. Tiff unbuttoned the right sleeve of her blouse and carefully cuffed it up past her elbow. She put her arm in the middle of the table, her fingers spread apart waiting for an opponent.

"What's the going bet? Fifty? A hundred?"

Harley looked up at Wife-Beater who was as stunned as he was.

"Fifty," said Harley. "Don't worry. He's limp-wristed and I'm sure he'll go easy on you."

Harley's entourage broke out into roaring laughs when she pulled the bills from her wallet. People scooted down the bench to make room for Wife-Beater to take his place at the table. Another greasy biker who reeked of cigarette smoke stepped up and clasped his hand over both of theirs as they settled into position.

"Three, two..." On 'one' the man let go and took a step back.

As she anticipated, instead of making a move the man toyed with her. Tiff made a half-hearted attempt to force the man's arm to the table, yet it barely moved. More bouts of laughter broke out as he lifted his other hand to his mouth and mocked a yawn.

The color leached from the bar—not that it was particularly vibrant, to begin with. While she continued to pull against his massive forearm, she reached out and forged a connection with his metacarpophalangeal joints—the knuckle where the hand meets the fingers. The MCP joints ground into one another and the man yelped in pain. The muscles in his arm relaxed and Tiff brought his wrist within inches of the tabletop. His hand swung down from his face and gripped the side of the table but refused to let go.

There were murmurs and quiet gasps from the table. And then Harley yelled out, "You're going to let a girl beat you, pussy?"

The others laughed.

A shiver overtook Tiff's body. Her vision clouded and the rest of the bar faded away as waves of heat radiated through her body. She felt nothing as her hand slammed to the table. He tried to pull away, but her fingers held firm.

"What the hell?" The big man shook his hand side-to-side trying to free himself from her grasp. "She's burning up."

Tiff became aware of her surroundings again. She relaxed her fingers and Wife-Beater fell backward. Her eyes fluttered shut as another aftershock overtook her. The gratitude sure as hell wasn't from her arm-wrestling opponent. Gregg and Bryce must have finally been reunited.

Wife-Beater stood up and reached for the bill on the table. She beat him to it, placing her hand atop his.

"Double or nothing?" That was all the cash she had, but the chances were slim the universe would cheat her out of another win. She hoped.

He stared at the fairy while rubbing his hand. When his buddies started clucking like chickens he sat back down.

They clasped hands once again. The look in his eyes told her he wouldn't go easy on her. Tiff straightened her back and adjusted accordingly. She fell into the same trance-like state as before and changed her grip several times to stall.

Tendrils of bone the width of a hair snaked out from his elbow and spine. They wrapped themselves around the man's ulnar and vagus nerves, respectively. Once they were in place, she sat still.

"Three... Two... One..."

A wisp of bone impinged the large man's ulnar nerve—the same one responsible for the 'funny-bone' reflex. In an instant, Tiffemory pinned his numb hand to the table, released her grip, and stood in a single fluid motion. She released the tendril of bone wrapped around the nerve and let it slither back into place.

To her surprise, the entire table was silent. She held her hand out.

"Pay up. And I'd appreciate it if you'd mind your manners for the rest of the night."

Wife-Beater slowly got to his feet, but he didn't make a move for his wallet. His eyes fixated upon her and narrowed.

"She did something to my arm," he said while repeatedly clenching and relaxing his fist.

The rest of the men got to their feet and closed a circle around her.

Even with her powers, Tiff knew she had no chance of stopping them all. But she wasn't going to just stand by idly. She directed the second offshoot of bone she'd prepared. This particular trick was one she hadn't tried before. The lasso began to cinch around his vagus nerve. She took it slow, after all, she didn't want to permanently paralyze the man.

The big biker got out of her face and looked down at the wet spot spreading across the front of his jeans.

Harley and the rest of the gang broke into raucous laughter.

Tiff put her head down. As she ducked out of the circle of bikers, she collided with another patron. A man in cutoff jean shorts, a short-sleeved dress shirt, and a tie decorated with vintage movie monsters fell backward. The pair of crutches in his hands went in opposite directions.

"I see you're making friends, Tiff," Joshua said with a groan from the floor.

"Shit. I should have known she was one of yours," Wife-Beater said, retrieving the crutches and helping Joshua to his feet. "But they're usually much greener around the edges. What the hell happened to you?"

"I tripped over my cat coming down the stairs."

"Get rid of that damn thing already," said Harley. "No self-respecting man should ever own a cat."

Tiff looked at Harley and then at the scrawny, pale counterfeiter. Like most of the bar's patrons, Joshua's forearms bore numerous tattoos. Only, his were significantly less fearsome. A blotchy, plush dinosaur in front of a roaring hearth didn't command the same presence as Satan's horned head. Joshua looked as out of place here as she did. Though, to be fair, he didn't look like he belonged anywhere.

"You all know each other?" she said.

Joshua nodded.

"They're rough around the edges, but not as hard as they look. I helped one of Harley's friends a while back. He's good people."

"Hang on," Tiff said, pointing at the large biker. "Your name's actually Harley?"

The man laughed. "I don't even own a bike."

Tiff turned back to the man she'd been arm wrestling.

"Don't tell me your name's Wife-Beater."

He laughed. "No, my parents weren't that cruel. It's Mark."

Mark reached into his pants and pulled out a wallet attached to a long chain. From it, he withdrew a fifty and a few smaller bills.

"Here. Take what I owe you."

Tiff shook her head. "It wouldn't be right. I cheated."

The man shrugged his shoulders and smirked.

"You still managed to best a man twice your size. A bet's a bet. And I deserve it for picking on a little girl." He held the money out again and Tiff stuffed it into her purse. "I imagine you've got things to discuss. If you'll excuse me, I need to go home and get a change of pants."

"Yeah... Sorry about that." Tiff said as the man walked past her.

Joshua led the way to a table near the door. Once they took a seat the bartender arrived with two glasses. Another Shirley Temple for Tiff, and something a lighter shade of pink for Joshua. She fumbled for her wallet, but Cary gave her a dismissive waved and retreated to his post behind the bar.

"Thanks for meeting on such short notice. I wasn't sure you'd come. I know you prefer to keep a low profile."

"Only a fraction of my clients are Outsiders. And believe me, I do my best to keep tabs on every one of them. I've been meaning to reach out to you for a while now. I've heard about the kids you've rescued."

"Oh..." Tiff looked over her shoulder to the table at the back of the bar. "How about them? Are any of those guys Outsiders? Or just your muscle?"

Joshua shook his head. "No, they're just acquaintances." He lowered his voice to a whisper. "And believe it or not, Mark's a cop."

Tiff's eyebrows rose. "And he's okay with what you do?"

"Well, not a real cop. He works undercover with Vice. He understands how the laws often work against good people and occasionally throws work my way."

"As long as we're sharing secrets... Should we talk about what happened to your leg? You don't get a spiral femur fracture from falling down a set of stairs."

"I'm not sure how they found me, but someone showed up on my doorstep a few days ago. I told them I don't do walk-ins."

"They kept pushing?"

"They offered way too much money for no-questions-asked IDs." Joshua shook his head. "I politely informed them I wasn't in the business of hooking up kids with wine coolers or getting them into clubs.

"Let's just say that their response was less than enthusiastic. Since then, I've decided to take a bit of a hiatus."

"That bad, huh?"

"Trust me, I know how to take a hint. They trashed my place and you've seen my leg. The guy barely even touched me."

Tiff sat up straighter. Joshua was more lanky than large but was in the prime of his life and, otherwise than his leg, healthy as a horse. Still, he was smart and should have been able to handle himself in a fight.

"It was just one guy?"

"Well no. There were two of them. But the one was a monster." He held his hand up. "Not a literal monster, mind you, but he did this with his bare fists."

Tiff took a big gulp of the drink in front of her, licked her lips, and looked down at a circular water mark on the table. From all the medical texts she'd read she knew such a break wasn't possible without a significant amount of force twisting in opposite directions. Short of being hit with a car—or some kind of barbaric method of torture—it shouldn't have been possible. It was another sign pointing toward Jeck's involvement. She looked back up, a frown dominating her face.

"Why didn't you go to the hospital? I'm not even sure how you're walking."

"Stubborn, I guess. It's healing on its own, granted a lot slower than I hoped."

"Wait, you're not..."

"Like you? Nah." Joshua shook his head and looked a little saddened. "Half at most, maybe a third. I can't say I paid enough attention in high school to remember the chapter on genetics. Anyway, I can't do the kinds of things you can. I have to admit, a part of the reason I agreed to meet was purely selfish."

The fairy smiled. "It's okay, I'd be honored." Tiff left her seat and knelt on the floor beside him.

"May I?" she asked, holding her hands just above his leg. While she could have made a connection to him from where she'd been sitting, it was always easier and safer to do things with physical contact. Plus, it was somehow less of an affront to the powers that be and thus, took less of a toll on her anchor.

When Joshua nodded, she lightly touched his skin and snapped her eyes shut. The jagged edges of his bones came into her mind's eye like a jigsaw puzzle. She reached out, feeling the edges of each before interlocking them again. The two bones called out to each other and responded, fusing into one long piece again.

Joshua cleared his throat and shifted uncomfortably as her hands roamed up and down the length of his thigh.

Even after removing her hands the warmth of the young man's skin remained with her fingertips. It crawled up her forearms and settled in her chest. Her breathing quickened and she had to reach out for the table leg for support. When the feeling passed, Tiff stood and returned to her seat.

"Stick with the crutches for another couple of weeks. The bone's healed as if no fracture had ever occurred. However, I can't do a thing about any tissue or muscle damage caused along the way. A little rehab would probably go a long way."

"I can't thank you enough," the counterfeiter said with a tear in his eye. "Now, tell me how I can repay you."

Tiff pulled the two ID cards from her purse and slid them across the table.

"That wasn't one of the guys who attacked you, was it?"

Joshua picked up Charles Weston's driver's license and shook his head.

"No. I've never seen this man before. Your case is related to my visitors?"

"There's a good chance. What can you tell me about the other card?"

He dropped Weston's license and picked up the other ID.

"Grace is the name of my parent's dog. This girl doesn't look like a Grace."

"So —"

"If you're asking whether it's fake, it is. And it isn't one of mine." He turned the card on its side and held it closer to his face. "I can tell you the schmuck who made it, though. He signs his work." Joshua held the card flat in front of her.

Tiff scratched her head. "What am I looking at?"

"If you look closely, there's a series of lines and dots along the edge. It spells out 'Allip' in binary. His work's not bad, he's just unscrupulous and a bit vain."

"Allip?"

Joshua sighed. "It's the name of an incorporeal creature from Dungeons and Dragons. He thinks he's being witty using it as his moniker. He hasn't learned the finer points of staying under the radar."

"Unless I'm mistaken, it sounds like you know who he is."

He smiled. "You can find Brandon Chavez at his family's dry-cleaning business downtown. I'll give you the address."

"Thanks."

Tiff swirled the ice around in her glass.

"There's something you're not telling me."

She set the glass back down. "I hope I'm wrong, but I have a feeling I know who's trying to run you out of business. If everything goes well, I'll get him out of the way again. I'll let you know when things go back to normal, but feel free to hit me up if you need any help with anything in the meantime."

"I usually point those guys at the abusive boyfriends," Joshua said gesturing toward Harley and Mark's group. "They're a pretty effective deterrent. But I'll keep you in mind."

Tiff said goodnight, pocketed the scrap of paper with the cleaner's address, and then headed to her car. The gravel in the lot crunched beneath her feet. On the way to the car, she noticed a figure sitting in the driver's seat of a car parked across the street. The bar was in a predominantly industrial section of town. The buildings surrounding the bar were all warehouses and the only other cars nearby belonged to The Derelict's patrons.

Tiff skirted past her car and peeked over her shoulder just long enough to check for northbound traffic. That glance was enough to confirm her suspicion. The dark figure slipped out of his car and fell into step behind her. The safest bet was to go back to the bar. But she wanted to know who he was.

Tiff walked three blocks and then let go of her purse and let it fall to the street. The figure dropped back when she bent down to pick it up. During that time, she also got a bead on her tail's skeletal structure.

She targeted the tibia bone in both her purser's legs. As she continued forward, she focused on pinching out sharp spurs of bone. They swept back and forth like little windshield wipers, cleaving paths through connective muscle tissue. From a couple of dozen paces behind, she heard the man gasped out in pain. Tiff smiled briefly. If she made a break for it, she could easily lose him and circle back to the car. Though, much like retreating to the bar, it wouldn't reveal the man's identity.

Tiffemory put her head down and forged ahead at a casual pace. At the end of the block stood the large, illuminated sign of a waffle house. The fist-sized light bulbs attracted teenagers, second shifters, and moths alike. Not to mention wayward tooth fairies.

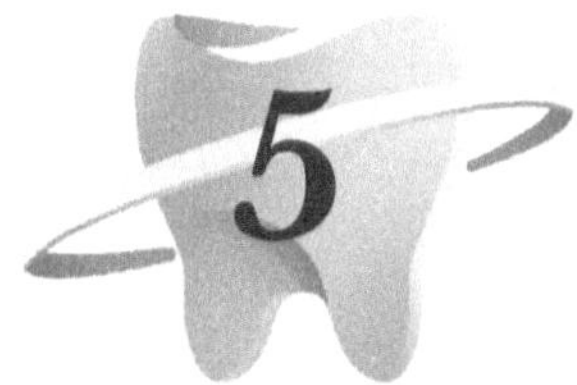

A bell on the door chimed as Tiff hurried inside and went to the back of the 24-Hour waffle house.

"Just sit anywhere," mumbled the young man behind the cash register as the fairy walked past.

Tiff chose a booth carefully, making sure to maintain a clear line of sight to the door.

A minute later a waitress in a red and white checkered dress uniform strolled up to the table. She placed a laminated menu in front of Tiff and then raised a black carafe.

"Coffee?"

"Please," Tiff said, turning over one of the cups sitting on a saucer in the middle of the table. She handed the menu back to the woman without looking at it. "A Belgian waffle, please. And could you bring me an empty bowl to go with it?"

"Sure thing, Hun." The waitress filled the cup with coffee and then set the pitcher in the middle of the table. "It'll just be a few minutes," she said before walking away.

Tiffemory poured four tiny cylinders of half-and-half into her coffee and started dumping in sugar packets. After emptying a dozen or so, a man in a pair of slacks and a windbreaker limped into the restaurant. She finally got a good look at her stalker.

The man was of average height with broad shoulders and an athletic build, probably in his early or mid-thirties. His dark hair was combed straight back, and a thin goatee framed his square jaw. The way he scanned the interior of the building hinted toward some sort of training—law enforcement or maybe a branch of the military. He inspected each customer in turn, sizing them up, and made notes of the exits.

When he met Tiff's eyes, he walked forward in long, even steps. His eyes narrowed with each footfall as he tried to hide the pain in his aching shins. The way he carried himself was familiar too. His left hand lingered closer to his belt than his right with each stride. He probably had a holster hidden on his left hip beneath the jacket.

The red plastic coating on the booth in front of her faded to gray as she took inventory of any noticeable weaknesses. The bones in his left arm were smooth but bore telltale signs of a decade-old fracture. If he were dumb enough to reach for his weapon, he'd never clear it from the holster.

The man came to a stop in front of her table.

"Mind if I join you, Tiffemory?"

Since he was following her, it came as no surprise that he knew her name. She scrutinized his face and drew blanks. He wasn't a past client. As far as she knew, she'd never met him before.

"As long as you tell me why you've been following me."

Even without physically touching him, there was a faint warmth radiating off the man. Whoever he was, he was grateful to her for something. Tiff relaxed her power as the man slid into the booth and unzipped his windbreaker. Beneath was a navy-blue Atlanta Police Department uniform.

"So, what can I help you with..." Tiff leaned forward to read the bronze nameplate. "Officer J. Cooper?"

"I'm off duty. You can call me Jasper."

Tiff settled back against the booth as the waitress returned to the table. She set down her waffle, an empty bowl, and a small jug of syrup.

"Sorry, I didn't know you were expecting company. Can I get you anything, officer?"

He smiled, revealing the dimples on his cheeks. "I'll just help myself to some coffee."

Tiff beat the waitress to the carafe and filled his cup. The woman gave a toothy smile, made a mark on her pad, and set off to check on her other tables. After pushing the cup toward Jasper, Tiff sawed off a quarter of the waffle and placed it into the empty bowl. The bottle of syrup gurgled as she upended it and drowned the waffle.

"I hope you don't mind if I eat while my food's warm."

"No," the officer said as the pool of syrup grew deeper. "Go ahead."

Jasper took a moment to watch Tiff shove soggy bites of waffle into her mouth before continuing.

"I've noticed an interesting trend."

"Oh?" she said, syrup dribbling down her chin.

"There's been an above-average number of missing person cases solved in the last few months. What's even more suspicious is that none of them had police involvement. Out of curiosity, I talked with several of those families. They all mentioned your name.

"I asked around and found a few officers familiar with your name. One of them told me she occasionally forwards your contact information along to the families of missing people."

"Missing persons are Greenstone Investigation's specialty," Tiff said in between mouthfuls. "And I'm good at what I do."

"Except for the fact that you're a missing person in your own right. I did a background check on you. Until a couple of years ago, you didn't exist. Which makes me wonder whether you're in WITSEC or are using a fabricated identity."

"If either of those were the case—and I'm not saying they are—it wouldn't be in my best interest to talk about it." Tiffemory smiled and took a sip of her vaguely coffee-flavored sugar. "If you had something to charge me with, I'd be at the station. So why are you following me?"

"I'm not here in an official capacity because I'm not sure you've done anything wrong. You seem to be doing good, to be honest, but something is off about you." He took a sip of his black coffee. "For example, seeing you hang around that seedy dive bar."

Tiff set her fork down. She tried to think back to The Derelict and then to the airport. She couldn't recall seeing him in either location, but she hadn't been looking.

"How long have you been following me?"

"I wasn't following you."

"If you knew that I was at the bar, you were."

"It's a long, boring story," he said.

"Good. I love stories. You can tell it while I eat."

Jasper bit his lower lip and then shrugged. "As a child, I always remembered my grandfather listening to a police scanner instead of the radio. I thought it was the neatest thing and it was what ultimately drove me toward a career in law enforcement. It wasn't until I was much older that I understood the reasoning behind it. My grandfather was a criminal. It didn't mean he was a bad person, mind you, he just made stupid choices.

"Grandpa passed a few years ago and left me his old police scanner in his will. I installed it in my car to carry on his tradition. Anyway, I was in the neighborhood when I heard the call go out about the old motel tonight. Imagine my surprise when I recognized your car parked across the street."

"That was a pretty personal story. It makes me wonder why you shared it with me."

"To make a point, I suppose. With a limited perspective, it can be difficult to discern good from evil or right from wrong." Jasper took another long drink of coffee. "You probably don't recall, but I was one of the responders when you rescued two girls from a construction site."

"Those girls' names are Mallory and Kate."

Jasper nodded.

"Look, I'm grateful for what you're doing, but something's not right. No offense, I find it difficult to believe that a hundred-pound woman incapacitated three human traffickers on her own. And aside from your lack of history, your business seems shady as well. Greenstone Investigations has no website and operates out of a supply closet.

"On top of that, the John Doe we arrested that night disappeared from jail a couple of days later. And by that, I don't mean he got out on a technicality or escaped. He was in his cell one minute and then gone the next."

Tiffemory licked the syrup from her lips again but said nothing. That man in question was Jeck. He was an Outsider—another tooth fairy. After rescuing the girls, she injected him with silver nitrate. It expedited the decay of his anchor and ultimately banished him back to Fae. She did her best to fight back a smile at the memory. Hopefully, it hurt.

"Something tells me you can explain more about that."

Tiff shrugged and shoved another dripping waffle segment into her mouth.

"I shared a story with you. Maybe you can share what you do with all the teeth you collect." Jasper looked her dead in the eyes.

Tiff froze mid-chew.

"I hear you've been telling clients you can extract DNA from their children's old, crumbling teeth. Which is a load of bullshit. A forensic expert could use it to identify a body, but unless you're cloning them, there's no way a tooth could lead you to a missing kid."

"You wouldn't believe me if I told you," she said after swallowing. "Besides, does it matter if it gets their children back?"

The officer sipped his coffee again.

"I had another reason for seeking you out."

Tiff raised an eyebrow. "Oh?"

"Nancy was going to call you in the morning, but since I've got you here... Someone came into the precinct this afternoon requesting help with a missing person. Only he refused to file a police report. He wanted to know what his *other* options were."

Her heartbeat raced but she tried to keep her cool. "Did you give him my information?"

"No," the detective said, shaking his head. "At the risk of sounding like a horrible person, he creeped me out. He had some sort of deformation—tumors protruding from his knuckles. But that wasn't what gave me pause. He was creepy in a way that's hard to put into words."

Tiff put her forearms on the table and leaned forward. She didn't recall anything wrong with his hands, but it had to be Jeck. The rogue tooth fairy was back and looking for revenge.

"Can you describe him? His face?"

"I can do you one better. After he left, I pulled up footage from the security cameras and printed an image. It's a little grainy because I zoomed in, but it's passable."

Jasper reached into his front shirt pocket and pulled out a paper folded in quarters. He passed it across the table.

"I wrote down the number he left on the back of the paper."

Tiff carefully unfolded the paper. The man in the picture was not Jeck. The proportions of his face weren't right to be a fairy. His nose was too broad, his cheekbones too high, and his jaw too square.

"You don't recognize him. You were expecting Mallory's kidnapper, weren't you?"

Tiff dropped the paper and studied the flakes of gold in Jasper's deep brown eyes. If she didn't know any better, she'd swear he had some Outsider blood in him.

"You're quite adept at reading people. Do you want to go down this rabbit hole?"

The detective sat up a little straighter and eyed her quizzically. "I'd be at home enjoying a beer and a recap of today's sports if I didn't."

"The name of Mallory's kidnapper is Jeck. He's an Outsider—what you'd call a tooth fairy, to be precise." She ignored his chuckles and continued. "Before getting the girls out of the building, I injected him with silver nitrate to make sure he wouldn't hurt—"

"You did what?!"

Tiff didn't bother finishing the sentence. She sat back and waited to see how he processed what little information she'd given him.

His eyes narrowed and he moved his head in what barely registered as a shake. "Jesus. You're serious. Is that why you're collecting teeth? You think you're the damn Tooth Fairy and you're hunting down other rogue fairies?"

"I usually only hunt down normal scum. Jeck is the only rogue fairy I've come across. And the injection was a temporary solution at best. I had a feeling he'd be back eventually."

"Back from where, pray tell?"

"The alternate reality we came from."

Jasper sighed loudly. "I don't know why I asked."

"It took mankind a few thousand years to develop the automobile, but less than a dozen more to master flight. And now you're well on your way to leaving the solar system. But you're still ages away from traveling to alternate realities or planes of existence."

"You're telling me the multiverse theory popularized by both Marvel and DC is real?"

"I'm not familiar with either of those theoretical physicists, but yes," Tiff said, nodding. "That's why you couldn't figure out how Mallory's kidnapper escaped from jail. Outsiders rely on something to keep themselves anchored here. Without it, they can't stay. It's like a splinter too deep to remove by hand. Your body knows it's a foreign object and eventually pushes it out."

"Listen. You're one hell of a storyteller but I think the stress is getting to you." Jasper threw a couple of bills onto the table for his coffee and started to slide out. "Have a good night."

Before he could slide out of the booth, Tiffemory placed her hand atop his.

"Cuff me."

"Excuse me?" Jasper said.

"You're still in uniform, so I presume you have a pair of handcuffs. Cuff me and I'll prove to you that I'm a tooth fairy."

"Escaping from cuffs makes you a tooth fairy? I've seen people do it before," he said as he slapped the metal bands around her wrists. "It's always because of improper application. You can't get out of a pair of handcuffs by dislocating your thumb. No matter what Hollywood tells you."

Jasper clicked the shackles an additional two times bringing the metal snug against her skin.

"I'm sorry if they're uncomfortable. Let me know when I've proven my point and I'll take them off."

Tiff smiled and shut her eyes. A barely visible wisp of bone from her Radius pushed through her skin. It slipped up and over the edge of the cuff and then into the keyhole. A second later, the right shackle popped open. She repeated the same process with the left.

Jasper shook his head. "How did you…"

The fairy looked around to see if any other patrons were paying attention. She dropped her napkin and suspended it using the thin wire of bone.

"Tooth fairies aren't what you think. We can manipulate bone. I could have just as easily shifted around the bones in my hands and slipped free. Though that hurts like hell since we don't have any control over muscle tissue or ligaments."

Jasper sat silent for a few minutes. His eyes roamed the space of the table without really focusing on anything.

Tiffemory absorbed the thread of bone back into her wrist and placed the napkin back into her lap.

"So, you're more of a bone fairy then," he said, finally looking back up.

"To be fair, we don't call ourselves anything. The whole tooth fairy thing is something you invented. Though if anything, I prefer that nomenclature."

"So. What's the deal with the teeth then?"

She smiled.

"It's a symbolic thing. I can establish a connection between myself and someone else using their tooth. A piece of bone works as well, but people generally tend to object to handing that over."

"Alright, I'll bite..." Jasper sighed. "No pun intended. How do you do this?"

"Once I swallow the tooth—"

Jasper coughed and spat half a mouthful of coffee onto the table. "Sorry," the officer said, blotting coffee off the front of his uniform and the table with napkins.

Tiff laughed. "That's okay. It's just as unpleasant as you imagine. Especially when it's been sitting in a plastic bag in mom's underwear drawer for a decade.

"Anyway, once the tooth is a part of me, I'm able to attune to the same wavelength of the owner so to speak. This lets me follow the established connection back to the source."

While Jasper sat back in the booth and tried to process things Tiff took the opportunity to finish the few remaining bites of her waffle. He raised an eyebrow and leaned forward.

"So, you could find Jimmy Hoffa if you could get ahold of one of his baby teeth?"

"As long as I'm nearby and act on it quickly enough. The link can only be maintained for eight hours at most and is only reliable over a handful of miles. Is he another local kid that went missing?"

Jasper cocked his head to the side. "Jimmy Hoffa?" He watched her for a moment and then said, "You don't know who Jimmy Hoffa is?"

"No. Should I?"

"Never mind, it was a bad joke. I must be crazy for entertaining this," he mumbled. "Okay. Say I choose to believe you. Why are you telling me all this?"

She shrugged.

"The same reason you opened up and shared the story about your grandfather. Plus, you're sharp and it would benefit me to have a connection within law enforcement I can trust and who understands things. For starters, yesterday I rescued another girl from a trafficker. I have some leads to follow up on and I imagine you can provide that information."

Jasper raised a finger to interject, but Tiff kept talking.

"More importantly, though, Jeck's more dangerous than you could understand. He wouldn't hesitate to do much worse than giving you shin splints."

His lips pursed and eyebrows drew together.

"I'm sorry about that, by the way," Tiff said with a frown. "I thought you were one of his lackeys. I'm glad I didn't have to revisit the previous injury to your left ulna."

Jasper said, putting down his coffee cup and pushing it into the center of the table. "I think I'm going to need something a bit stronger."

"I know it sounds cliché, but I'm one of the good ones."

"How many of you are there out there?"

"I don't know," Tiff said after a long pause. "But Jeck's the first one who I've come across with malintent." She quickly diverted her gaze from the police officer's face down to her coffee.

"Shit. Are you implying that there are things other than fairies out there?"

"It seems short-sighted to believe I'm the only thing that can cross over into your reality," Tiffemory said with a big smile. "One case at a time, detective."

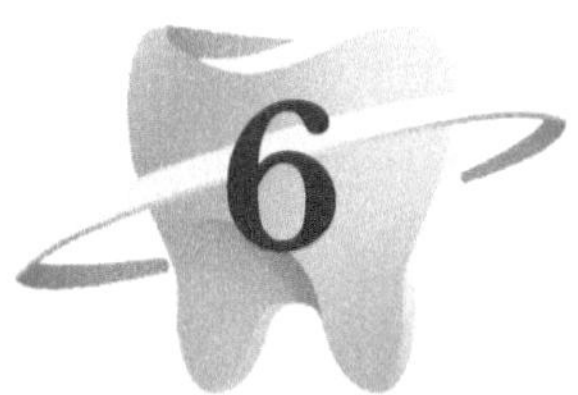

Tiff pulled up in front of the bungalow with faded white siding she called home. After scooping up all her belongings she walked down the long driveway. At the rear of the house, down several steps was her basement apartment. The motion light above the door came on, illuminating a neatly handwritten note taped to the door.

Tiff,
I've gone to bed. I figured you wouldn't mind if I let myself in and put a slice of pie in the refrigerator for you. Have a good night.
Dolores

She smiled and pulled down the note. Dolores was her landlord of sorts. The old woman was the homeowner who lived on the first floor of the house. Despite an age difference of almost half a century, the two hit it off when introduced a few months ago.

When Tiff first arrived in Atlanta she lived and worked in a woman's shelter. It was honest work that provided small opportunities to bolster her anchor. With a little help from her natural gifts, she subdued a psychotic father trying to reclaim his son. Her impressed supervisor offered up the basement apartment that had recently lost its tenant. Tiff kept an eye on Dolores and helped with odd jobs around the house in exchange for room and board.

The fairy stepped inside, slipped off her shoes, and closed the door. Much like her office, the basement was cozy and not very spacious. Excluding the unfinished area housing the furnace and storage, she was left with roughly four hundred square feet of living space. Not that Tiff needed any more than that. After all, she hadn't had a lifetime to accumulate crap.

When she tossed her purse on the bed her phone and wallet came tumbling out. She started to cram the items back inside when the folded printout caught her eye. Despite Jasper's warning, and her instincts, she wondered if the person truly required help. Tiff removed the paper from her purse and unfolded it. Try as she might, the face didn't trigger any memories. Despite the hour, she flipped it over and dialed the number.

The line connected without as much as a ring. In place of a hello, a bloodcurdling scream came through the speaker followed by uncomfortable silence. Tiff's heart pounded and she froze. A few seconds later there was a beep. She sighed in relief. It was only a recording. She hung up the phone and put her hand to her chest. This was one of the reasons she chose not to advertise her services publicly.

Tiff took one last glance at the photo before folding it back up again. Someone was screwing with her, but she wasn't sure it was Jeck now. There had to be a connection to a prior case. Perhaps it was an angry ex-husband or father who lost their child. If that were the case, they'd likely have a criminal record, or at least be noted in a file. Not to mention a lot of nerve to show their faces around the police department...

While she still had her phone out, she copied Jasper's contact information from the business card he gave her before leaving. She plugged her phone in to charge and readied herself for bed. After slipping into a tee shirt and shorts, she let her hair down. The piece of Gareth's bone had a special place on the nightstand where it would be within arm's reach.

As exhausted as she was from the whirlwind of a day, there was a certain appeal to staying up for a bit. Her anchor had gone from one extreme to another today. As much as it allowed her to remain in Atlanta, it also rooted her to a part of home. And for whatever reason, it often spurred unpleasant visions or memories.

The basement apartment didn't have a television, but what it did have was a large bookshelf. Tiff's interest lay in non-fiction: particularly scientific journals and medical textbooks. She walked to the large bookshelf near the door and inspected the spines of the books. After a moment of deliberation, she selected an out-of-date medical publication from the top of a stack of magazines.

She took a seat and then sprang back up again. There was pie. As Dolores promised, a plastic wrap-covered plated awaited her in the middle of the refrigerator. Tiff smiled and grabbed the plate holding nearly an entire quarter of a pie. She lifted it and took a deep sniff. Apple.

Tiff climbed onto her trundle bed, pulled her legs underneath her bottom, and leaned against the cool concrete wall. Even though she'd put down a waffle an hour ago, she couldn't resist. She dug in and flipped through the magazine in search of something interesting. When she found no articles about musculoskeletal issues, she considered tossing it aside in favor of another. However, something else caught her eye: a feature detailing a new surgical alternative to open-heart surgery. Instead of accessing the heart via the ribcage, valve repairs could be completed via a small incision near the groin.

By the time she finished with the article, so too was the pie. She put the plate aside, slid beneath the covers, lazily flipped through the magazine, not absorbing any information. Eventually, the magazine slipped from her grasp and fell to the floor. The fairy succumbed to sleep. The surface of the bone chopsticks on the nightstand beside her bubbled and liquified. A puddle grew on the nightstand.

First, the bust of a woman rose from the white liquid. Following it came a pair of fairy wings so thin and detailed they were almost translucent. Finally, the torso and legs of the figure emerged until the puddle was depleted. The five-inch-tall statue perched of a 'traditional' fairy was the original form of the chopsticks she carried with her everywhere. It was her only treasured possession—a gift from her husband Gareth.

Even as exquisite a piece of craftsmanship the statue was, the intrinsic value was far higher than its monetary value. The figure was a literal piece of her husband. Part of his Femur, she presumed. It was the ultimate expression of love a fairy could give to another.

The statue's emergence brought about the nightmarish vision as she'd feared.

Tiff closed her eyes and stepped through the shimmering portal, leaving Atlanta behind. Sun streamed through tiny gaps in the foliage of the broad oaks. Before opening her eyes, she took a deep breath. Instead of hints of car exhaust, the air was crisp, floral, and earthy. It must have rained since she was away.

Her eyes snapped open when she detected a hint of something else in the air. The metallic scent of blood.

A dozen guards from the village stood around her with their massive bone spears at the ready. Tiff's arms fell to her side and the picture book and candies she purchased for her daughter fell into the mud.

"What's going on? What happened?"

One of the guards lowered his weapon and came to her side. He gripped her arm and ushered her past a face-down body of a man dressed all in black. Tiff glanced over her shoulder as they passed. Blood coated the tall grass in a broad swath around the body. Only there was too much of it to be from a single source.

"What happened here? Who is that?"

The older fairy said nothing and continued to guide her from the clearing in the woods.

It was clear she wasn't going to receive any answers to her questions, so Tiff fell quiet. The guard released her arm and waited for her to start down the path. She emerged from the woods to find nearly every member of the village gathered around the open door of her cabin.

She sprinted inside, shrugging off hundreds of hands reaching out to comfort her.

"Gareth! June!"

When there was no response, she rushed from room to room in search of her family. She saw the body of June first, lying in her bed. A shroud of ivory encompassed her body. At least, everything but her gray, exsanguinated face.

The white fabric darkened in spots as a storm of tears fell. Tiff dropped to her knees, kissed June's forehead, and then whispered a prayer in her name. The fairy rose and repeated the sentiment for the other love of her life.

Their deaths were her fault. When she left Fae, something piggybacked in behind her.

Operating on autopilot, her feet carried her through the cabin. She grabbed Gareth's statue, the one thing dearest to her besides her family, and stumbled outside.

Faceless peers supported Tiff when she collapsed. Instead of helping get her upright again, they pinned her to the ground. The statue lifted out of her hands, propelled by tiny wings flitting like a hummingbird's. It twisted midair and stretched into a wide choker. The bone snapped forward like a striking snake, wrapping around her neck and squeezing.

Tiff rolled over in bed, coughing and choking. Her teary eyes settled upon the statue on the bedside table. She reached out to the object and held it close.

"I'm sorry," she said, planting a kiss on the top of the figure's head.

The statue shouldn't have been able to modify its shape without her conscious thought guiding it. And yet, every night the piece of bone transformed back to match Gareth's wedding gift. She could never decipher how he managed that feat. Part of her hoped he'd found a way to watch over her even in death.

The fairy statue was an odd choice for the token exchanged between mates. It was traditionally jewelry: bracelets, anklets, necklaces, and occasionally rings—the common marital bond among humankind. But Gareth embraced Tiff's infatuation with the reality parallel to theirs. And in turn, their interpretation of fairies.

Tiff placed the statue back on the nightstand and fluffed the pillow beneath her head. Gareth would be proud of everything she accomplished today. She'd set out to come to the aid of one child and ended up saving two.

On top of that, a potential ally in law enforcement landed in her lap. She wondered if she should have given him Weston's wallet. Jasper may have been able to use that information in some legal capacity. Though, she dumped a lot of things on him all at once. And it had yet to be seen whether she could put her faith in the man or not.

Even though the gratitude coming off him was palpable, something about the run-in bothered her. It was awfully coincidental, to say the least.

After another restless hour of dwelling on the past, she fell back into a restful sleep.

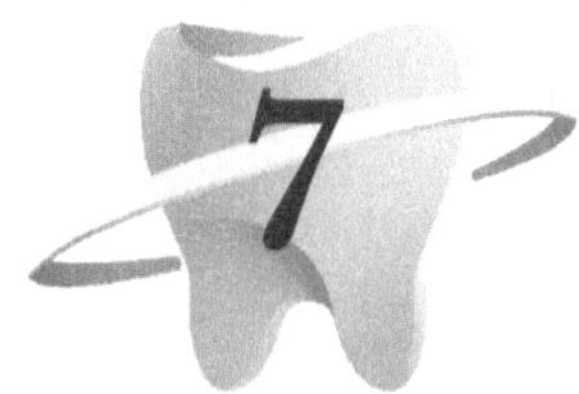

Tiff wiped a bead of sweat from her brow. It was only a quarter after seven and yet her car's black interior was already hot to the touch. The aging yellow Toyota's air conditioner worked sporadically. Unfortunately, today was not one of those days. Grumbling about it seemed petty. After all, there were no air conditioning units in Fae. However, her village didn't have a witty nickname like 'Hotlanta'.

She drove to the top of the hill and circled the cul-de-sac before pulling up to the curb. Weston's house—or at least the address listed on his license—was a two-story, red-brick colonial. It sat in a quiet neighborhood beside a compliment of other houses just as large. The property covered at least an acre and backed up to a wooded lot.

Her pastel green sundress swished about her knees as she exited the car. Tiff took a deep breath and savored the gentle breeze coming from the north. The smell of freshly manicured grass and lilac bushes trimmed into perfect spheres almost made her forget why she was here. Despite its outward appearance, the million-dollar estate in front of her belonged to a monster.

Flowering topiaries flanked the fairy as she stepped onto the porch. Before knocking, she let her vision blur and called upon her other senses. She swept her head from side to side and gave the property a quick once over. Something quadrupedal, likely a deer, frolicked in the woods behind the house. The house itself was empty. No one milled about the interior or sat in shackles within the basement. At least not anyone living.

Her original plan was to interrogate Weston on the spot. As a backup, she figured there could be something to gain from searching his place—or lying in wait for him. Tiff reached for the piece of bone in her hair to pick the lock. The hum of a US Postal truck coming up the hill made her reconsider.

Tiff stepped off the porch. Breaking in right now wasn't worth the risk. Her car was old, and while it only had a few rust spots, it still stuck out in this neighborhood. If she got arrested thanks to a nosy neighbor calling the police, she wouldn't be able to help anyone. Weston had to know she had his wallet. She was sure he was lying low somewhere else. If need be, she could always come back under the cover of night, park down the hill, and sneak in through the back door.

The fairy returned to her car and slid into the driver's seat. Before she could start the ignition, her phone rang. She dug the device out of her purse in a hurry. Very few people had her number. If it was ringing this early, it was probably an emergency.

Craig's number showed on the screen. The notification bar in the corner showed two missed calls. He must have called as soon as she left the car.

"Thank God you're there," Craig said, frantically. "Mallory's missing again."

Her vision blurred as the words sank in. The last shred of doubt as to who was behind the recent goings-on was gone. Dawn's kidnapping, running into Weston again, and the incident with Joshua's broken leg all pointed to Jeck. Mallory was the last girl Tiff had rescued from his clutches before sending the rogue fairy packing.

Tiff shook her head clear as Craig called out her name again.

"Tiff, are you there?"

"Yeah. Sorry, I'm here."

"I'm at the airport right now. They're about to close the boarding door without me."

There was a shuffling in the background and a muffled threat to have him arrested.

"I have to go. I'm texting you my ex-wife's address. Stacey's expecting you. Let her know I'll be there as soon as I can."

"I'm on my way, Craig. I—" The line clicked dead. "Promise I'll bring Mallory back again," she said to herself, lowering the phone.

When Tiffemory first met Craig Sanderson six months ago he came across as a corporate tool. However, he was a desperate corporate tool. After his daughter Mallory disappeared, somehow word of mouth brought him to her office. Regardless of whether Craig was a likable individual or even a good father, he needed her help. *Mallory* needed her help.

Not that she knew much about the man at the time, but in the weeks following the ordeal, Craig became a different person. While still a workaholic, he no longer threw his entire being into his work. Craig successfully salvaged his relationship with his daughter and ex alike. On top of that, he became Greenstone Investigation's unofficial corporate sponsor. Craig made sizable donations of both his time and money to put her where she was. She even had him to thank for being able to afford the very car she sat in, not to mention teaching her to drive it.

Tiff glanced back at Weston's monstrous house, put the car into drive, and sped to Stacey's house.

***

The street in front of the Abrahms' house wasn't what Tiff expected. There were no news vans, and more importantly, no flurry of police activity. The street was quiet, save for a woman jogging by with her dog. Their next-door neighbor sprayed newly planted grass while slurping from a coffee mug.

The front door of the blue split level opened the moment Tiff pulled in front of the house. A woman stepped outside and held the storm door open in anticipation of her arrival.

Stacey stood a full head taller than Tiff. A purple tank top and black yoga pants revealed a tight and lean physique. When she wiped away the occasional tear, her biceps bulged. Tiff couldn't help but think Craig's ex would have taken any of the bikers from the bar last night in a fair fight. It also became quite apparent how Craig had gotten the black eye the first time he'd showed up at her office.

The fairy grabbed her purse and hurried up to the house, shaking Stacey's outstretched hand when she offered it.

"I'm Tiff. I take it Craig told you I was coming?"

The woman nodded and forced a weak smile. "Yes, he did. I'm Stacey. Please come in."

The woman followed Tiff into the house but didn't stray from the doorway. She stared, scouring every inch of the fairy's face before quickly gazing down at her own trembling hands.

"Craig said you were responsible for bringing Mallory home..." She lifted her head again and gazed into Tiff's eyes. "Last time."

"That's right."

"Sorry, I don't mean to stare. I have a weird feeling we've met before."

"It's okay," Tiff said, shaking her head. "I get it all the time. I must have one of those faces. One of the perils of being pretty, I suppose," Tiff added, garnering an honest smile from her host.

Tiff stood awkwardly in the doorway and stole a glance around. The house bore an open floor concept: the entryway flowed naturally into both the den and the kitchen. Tiff swept her eyes across the floor and then the counter in the kitchen. The house was immaculate. There were no dirt or scuff marks from excess foot traffic or coffee cups piled up at the side of the sink.

"Forgive me if I'm blunt. Why haven't the police been by yet?"

"Craig told me they were a waste of time. He said you'd take care of everything."

Tiff closed her eyes and let out a long sigh.

"No offense, but your ex-husband's an idiot."

"I've been saying that for years." Stacey chuckled again and her stance relaxed a bit. "I'm sorry. We don't have to stand in the entryway. Come take a seat. Can I get you some water or something?"

Tiff shook her head and bent down to remove her shoes. Stacey waved her off.

"The floor is the least of my worries."

The women moved to the kitchen and took a seat at a square table nestled into the nook of a bay window.

Tiff grabbed the notebook from her purse, fished the pen out of the wire spiral, and opened it to a blank page.

"I'll do everything in my power to bring Mallory back home. First I need you to tell me everything you can."

Stacey sniffled and took a deep breath.

"This morning started like any other. I woke up, made a smoothie, and then went for a run. I was about to leave to teach a kickboxing class when I realized Mallory's car wasn't in the garage. She's not a morning person and it was too early for school. That was when I knew something was wrong.

"I've been calling her phone and it keeps going straight to voicemail. Only there's no personal greeting. The one exception was the first time I called this morning. Someone picked up but refused to say anything. Even after I screamed into the phone."

Tiff cocked her head. "You didn't hear anything at all? Or nobody said anything? There's an important distinction between the two."

"I could hear a faint whistling. Like it was part of a song or something."

Tiffemory froze and dropped the pen. That was Jeck alright. After she disabled two of Mallory's captors but before she could lead the way out of the building, Jeck showed up. The smug bastard announced himself by whistling a fairy lullaby.

"What is it? Does that mean something to you?"

"Did it sound like this?" Tiff pursed her lips together and blew gently. She cycled through five sharp notes that rose and fell in pitch and then changed octaves and repeated the process. The song was a portion of the Fibonacci sequence put to music. She'd heard it thousands of times from her mother and had probably whistled it thousands of times to June.

Stacy shook with excitement. "That's it! Does it mean something?"

The fairy bit her top lip, splitting the irritated patch of skin she always chewed on and trickling blood down her throat. This was her fault. She banished Jeck back to their reality but took no further actions to permanently deal with the problem. He waltzed right back to Atlanta, just as she knew he would.

The fairy lowered her head. "It means she's been taken by the same person as last time." She jumped when Stacey placed her hand atop her own. The woman's hand was freezing.

"Why is this happening again? Did she see something she shouldn't have? Please... I need to hear it straight."

Tiff pressed her tongue against the cut on her lip and fought to keep her eyes dry.

"This has nothing to do with Mallory," she said in almost a whisper. "It's about me." To Tiff's surprise, Stacey didn't move.

"I see..."

"I sent the man responsible for your daughter's kidnapping away. I foolishly thought it would end things. I'm sorry... I should have done more." Tiff tried to pull her hand back. To her surprise, Stacey held it in a death grip.

Tears flowed freely down Stacey's face. She sniffled and wiped them away with one hand, keeping hold of Tiff with the other. She swallowed.

"It's not your fault. We know you did everything you could." Stacey let out a little laugh. "Mallory only remembers bits and pieces from that night, but she has a vivid recollection of you beating the crap out of three grown men. If anyone is to blame, it's those scumbags. Or the police. We read about how one of them escaped while in their custody."

Tiff dried her eyes and met the woman's gaze again.

"Craig and I have every bit of faith in you. We know you'll get Mallory back again. And you already know who has her." Stacey shifted in her seat, let go of the fairy's hand, and sat up straighter in the chair.

"I almost forgot. I have the last of her baby teeth too. It's all dark and gross, but Craig said it will help you find her."

Tiff nodded. "Perhaps." She wiped her eyes again and picked up the pen. "Sorry, I guess it's not very professional to break down in front of a client."

Stacey smiled. "It's okay. If you were emotionless, I'd be concerned you weren't human."

"Who says I'm not?" She returned the smile and managed a quick laugh. "When was the last time you saw your daughter?"

"Thursday—Last night. We had dinner together and settled in the den in front of the television. Well, mostly I watched while she sat on the couch and fiddled with her phone."

"Do you two have a good relationship?"

"She's a teenager so of course, we have our differences but we're close. She knows she can come to me with anything that's on her mind. Craig has been making more of an effort to be in her life too."

"Any boyfriends in the picture?"

"None that she's mentioned."

"Have you ever caught her sneaking out of the house?"

"I'm pretty lenient when it comes to house rules. Her curfew is eleven during the week and midnight on the weekends. For the first four or five months following the incident, she only left the house for school and therapy sessions. She's starting to go out more frequently, but she and her friends tend to hang out here.

"But to answer your question, it's entirely possible. Craig bought her a car for her birthday back in April. And I'm a sound sleeper. A jet could buzz the house and I'd never wake up. I suppose I wouldn't even know if she has been sneaking out."

"I saw a security system keypad beside the door. Do you know whether it keeps logs?"

"I think so, but I'm not sure I know how to access them. I imagine Craig can do that when he gets here."

"Okay. I only have a few more questions to ask. Have you noticed anyone strange coming around or following you?"

"No, but I probably haven't been paying attention."

"Has there been anything, in general, that felt off? More solicitors coming to the door than usual, car accidents, or late-night calls with heavy breathing or hang-ups?"

Stacey shook her head.

"No feelings of being watched or someone with a familiar face you couldn't place?" Tiff smiled. "Other than mine."

"No. Nothing like that comes to mind."

"Okay. I'll move on then. Do you know if Mallory has kept in touch with Kate, the other girl... she was with that night?"

"Yeah. They still talk. Though her family has subsequently moved out of the state." Stacey's hand went to her mouth. "I hope she's okay."

"I'll follow up. Can you connect me with anyone else from her circle of friends? Maybe they know something more. Not that I'm suggesting she's intentionally keeping things from you, but you know kids. Even if you're close to your parents there are plenty of things you wouldn't open up about."

Stacey nodded.

"Mallory has a lot of acquaintances but there aren't many girls she's close to. I don't have most of their numbers. Though, I can put you in touch with her best friend Julie. I went to college with her mother, so our families are close. I can give you her contact information."

"I'd also like Mallory's cell number and the make and model of her vehicle along with the license plate number."

"Okay," Stacey said with another nod. She walked away from the table to fetch the requested information.

Tiff chewed on the cap of the pen and tried to determine if she missed anything. There were binders in her office with lists of scripted questions. It didn't seem prudent to stop for them when she knew exactly who was behind the kidnapping.

Either Jeck discovered Mallory's father was helping to finance Tiff's little 'war' against his empire or Mallory was simply the last girl she'd saved from his clutches. Either way, it seemed like a solid plan as far as revenge goes. Before she'd bested him and set the wheels in motion for his banishment, he'd given her an ultimatum. Work with him, get out of the way, or suffer. He was making good on his promise.

While Tiff didn't know much about the man, she could only presume he'd taken Mallory as a bargaining chip. The fact that he hadn't reached out to offer a trade meant he was toying with her. And it almost certainly meant that Mallory was alive. Or so she hoped.

Tiff's mind continued to spiral to a dark place. Since opening her PI business, she'd rescued a dozen or so kidnapped children. There was no way of telling which ones had been taken at the hand of Jeck's organization. Were there other signs she missed?

Stacey returned to the table and placed a lined sheet of paper on the table.

"There's Julie's number and address, Mallory's number, and everything for her car: make, model, color, VIN, etcetera."

She took a seat again, her hands cupped around a small circular tin decorated with a cartoonish image of a baby shark. After twisting the lid off, she gave the contents a little shake. Three small browning pieces of a tooth jostled from side to side.

"Mallory didn't stop believing in the Tooth Fairy until she was eight or nine." A smile cracked Stacey's lips as she recalled the memory. "She wasn't angry or disappointed we'd been lying to her. Instead, what bothered her was that we'd been throwing out something that was once a piece of her. For whatever reason, something compelled her to keep them. She'd already lost most of her baby teeth by that time, but Craig bought her this tin. I'd forgotten we had it until... You know."

She pressed the lid back onto the container and slid it across the table.

Tiff picked it up and placed it into her purse. She let her hand linger in the bag for a moment and then decided to share the image Jasper had provided. There was always the off chance that it may jog her memory.

"Is there any chance you recognize this man?" Tiff unfolded the paper and handed it across the table.

"No, he doesn't look familiar," Stacey said after scrutinizing the paper. "Is this the man who took her before?"

"No. I can't even say he's related to your daughter's disappearance. I just wanted to rule it out."

Tiff folded the paper back up and provided no further elaboration. Not that she *had* anything else to elaborate on. She angled her bag toward her and slipped the ID out of Weston's wallet. Keeping her thumb over the name and address, she held it out at arm's length in front of Stacey.

"How about this man?"

Stacey squinted. "That looks an awful lot like Charles Weston."

"You know him?" Tiff said, her eyes widening.

"Yeah. Well, not personally. He owns four or five restaurants around the Atlanta metropolitan area. Wait..." She licked her lips and swallowed a lump in her throat again. "Why do you have his driver's license? Is he involved somehow?"

Tiff's lips pulled together tight and she wished she'd done some research before showing off the picture. She decided to play the event down. No point in turning Craig or Stacey toward vigilante justice.

"I don't know that he's involved. I came across it while investigating something unrelated." She tossed it back into her purse, stood up, and pushed her chair in. "I think that's all for now."

Stacey walked Tiff to the door and embraced her.

"Thank you. I'm sure Craig will be in touch too when he lands." She paused for a moment and fidgeted with her fingers. "You never mentioned how much—"

"Nothing. Don't worry about that. But I do need one more thing from you."

"Name it."

"You need to contact the police and file a missing person's report. I know you think I'm a miracle worker, but you shouldn't discredit any other available resources."

"Okay..."

"If Craig gives you a hard time about it, he can take it up with me. I'll let you know as soon as I find something."

Tiff got into her car and waved goodbye as she drove off. While Julie's house was close and the next logical step, it would have to wait. It was too early unless she pulled the girl out of school. That was okay. She wanted to hit the office and do some research first.

Tiff pushed the door to her office open. The room wasn't an office in the traditional sense but more of a windowless cubby that used to be a janitor's closet in a past life. Despite Craig's numerous attempts to persuade her into a proper space, she resisted. Most of her work was done in the field and the rent was too cheap to pass up.

In the end, they reached a compromise. Craig hired a general contractor to spruce the place up. They removed exposed plumbing, touched up the drywall, hung new cabinets, and splashed fresh paint on everything. Her sponsor also hooked her up with a laptop and a desk and chairs that appropriately fit within the limited real estate. Last but not least, there was a custom placard with her name on the door. She suspected Craig kept the old sign—a piece of printer paper—and burned it.

She slumped into the ergonomic chair that still smelled of new leather and stared at the closed laptop. The research was her least favorite part of the job. She understood how useful computers could be, but it still didn't make her like them. Stumbling through the navigation system on her smartphone, opening texts, and making calls were manageable tasks especially with the voice-aided assistant.

Navigating endless seas of database results with the stupid little touchpad on the laptop was not her idea of a fun time.

Tiff knew a bit about the investigative process. When she wasn't busy tackling missing person cases, she was sneaking into lecture halls at Georgia Tech. She'd taken enough criminal justice, law, and physical therapy classes to earn a degree or two. At least if she'd paid for the classes.

But knowledge was one thing and experience another. It was impossible to get a private investigator's license without a hundred hours of experience working under another PI. Luckily, Joshua's handiwork falsified enough records to make that happen. Coupled with the fact that her usual clientele was able to supply a child's tooth, there was usually no need for any of the mundane investigations. That was why she always pushed to get the police involved.

She consulted the notes she took at Stacey's and made two lists on separate sheets of paper. The first was grunt work she could handle: double-checking Mallory's number, making sure her former clients were all okay, checking local impounds looking for Mallory's car, and delving into the background of the restaurateur.

The other list included things better suited for a more experienced hand: looking up property records of the Sunnyside Motel and probing more into Weston's background. She was curious whether he maintained ties to any charitable organizations—particularly shelters—and what other properties he owned.

Tiff grabbed the second list and went down the hall to consult her unofficial partner. Hazel Cummings worked for the small accounting practice a few doors over. Before Craig set her up, she piggybacked off her Wi-Fi and solicited her for minor IT issues. They became friends and Tiff ultimately gave her access to her PI credentials. This gave her the ability to search public records and whatever other databases she had authority to access.

But the old woman wasn't just a sexagenarian with a knack for tech. The grandmother of twelve raised six kids of her own. In the course of providing for her large family, she'd worked the gamut: wedding photographer, a paralegal, real estate agent, and a certified public accountant. When Tiffemory ran into something out of her expertise—anything more complex than the top result of a Google search—Hazel was happy to help. And despite offering to pay her for her time, Hazel always gave her assistance pro-bono.

Tiff pushed the glass door to the office open a crack and peeked in. For once, Hazel wasn't on the phone. The overweight woman in a flowery blouse looked up from her computer and waved the fairy forward.

"I know that look. Come... Let's see if I can help." Hazel put on the pair of glasses hanging from a beaded chain around her neck and glanced at the list. "Property investigations and 501c lookups. I thought for once you'd have something challenging for me. This is a piece of cake."

"To be honest, I'm not sure what I'm looking for. I think Weston's involved in something shady. I need to find out whether there's anything that proves it."

"I'll see what I can find. Will you be around? I should be able to get back to you in a couple of hours. Unless it's urgent."

"It's not that urgent," Tiff said glancing over at a coworker of Hazel's who was staring. "I need to move on my case one way or another. But first, I have about a hundred phone calls to make. I can check in before I leave."

"Alright. Well, be careful."

"I'm not leaving the building," the fairy said with a smile. "But I will."

Hazel knew enough about what Tiff did for a living to be concerned. No matter the circumstance, her parting words were always 'be careful'.

Tiff returned to her office and punched Mallory's number into her office phone. It went directly to a generic voicemail greeting. Her mouth turned down. She didn't know whether that meant the phone was off or the settings were changed. Tiff hung up and wheeled her chair over to the cabinet beside the south wall. From the bottommost shelf, she withdrew an ivory-colored box measuring about ten by twelve inches. The protective casing of bone responded to her touch, sliding away and gathering in a strip at the spine of the three-ring binder within.

She flipped the scrapbook open to the first page. Tucked within the plastic sheet was a piece of paper with notes and a photo of a young boy. Donny was her first case. It had no ties to human trafficking. It was much worse. Tiff closed her eyes and could still see the shaking boy in the trunk of the car parked outside the illegal gambling den. She gritted her teeth as another memory came to the surface.

Instead of calling the authorities, Tiff moved the child to her car and waited for the bastard that took him to return. After breaking both of his ankles she got a confession out of the man. He'd taken Donald from a nearby park and planned on trading the child to pay off debts to a known pedophile. She nearly lost it and crippled the man on the spot. Luckily, a bystander who saw her pull the child from the trunk earlier alerted the police.

She lingered on that page for a moment and touched the photo of the child. That night was the closest she'd come to killing someone.

Tiff went through the remaining pages one at a time remembering the faces of the angels she'd saved. When there was a possible link to Jeck's organization, she placed a colored sticky note. Aside from Mallory, she was left with six potential cases. She picked up the phone and dialed the first on the list.

"Mrs. Delgado? It's Tiffemory Greenstone."

"Who? Oh, Tiff! Good to hear from you. What can I do for you?"

Tiff couldn't help but smile as a warm, tingling sensation spread up her arms. It wasn't enough to recharge her battery so to speak, but the small resurgence of gratitude from the woman was more than welcome. And it did lengths to push the thoughts of Donny's case from her mind.

"I know you haven't heard from me in months and I hope this doesn't come off as creepy, but I wanted to call and see how Maria was doing."

"No, that's not weird at all. It's good to hear from you. Maria's fine. She's been under the weather the past few days but is finally perking up. She's downstairs playing. Do you want me to call her up to say hello?"

"No, I don't want to disturb her. I just wanted to let you know I've been thinking of your family. Have a good day."

"We will. Thank you and God bless. We'll never forget what you did for us."

Warmth spread from the fairy's arms up into her shoulders. Tiff had to wink away a tear as she ended the call.

She kept each subsequent call casual, a simple wellness check for each child. There was no reason to cause any additional alarm to any of the families. Every child was accounted for. She breathed a sigh of relief and smiled. This was something she'd have to make a habit of doing. The reminders of all the good she'd done were intoxicating.

After removing all the sticky notes from the binder, she closed it and placed it back on the shelf. Without a prompt, the bone spread outward until it enveloped the entire binder in a protective sheath.

Tiff lifted the lid of her laptop and waited for it to boot so she could attend to the next item—attempting to track down Mallory's car. When the machine finally started, she tapped out her query on the keyboard.

A map of Atlanta filled the screen. The city itself had a dozen impound lots, not to mention the outlying areas. She went through the list alphabetically, starting with All-Tow. Tiff rattled off the car's description to the receptionist and waited. When they couldn't confirm possession of the vehicle she moved to the next company.

Repossession officers and impound staff were not the friendliest individuals. A fight broke out in the background at one place, she was hung up on twice, and cussed at more than she cared to be. The calls ended with being on hold for twenty minutes only to have to repeat the information to someone else. What should have been a simple task turned into almost two hours of frustration with nothing to show for it.

Tiff set the phone down and rubbed her temples. The thought of having to call multiple police municipalities or tow yards in the surrounding towns made her want to pull her hair out. After staring at the computer screen for fifteen minutes, she crossed the task off the list. If Stacey followed her advice, Atlanta PD would be involved by now. Surely, they'd be doing the same thing she was, albeit more efficiently.

She cleared the search results and typed in 'Charles Weston Atlanta'. As she moved the cursor to the first link a knock came at the door. Tiff groaned in response.

"That bad, huh?" Hazel said, letting herself into the cramped office.

"I've been on the phone for the past three hours. It's starting to feel like it's been three years."

Hazel laughed and squeezed into a chair.

"I take it you're ready for some good news then... At least if you interpret no news as good news." She held a few loose sheets of paper up to her eyes and recapped what she dug up. "The Sunnyside Motel was foreclosed upon and seized by Wells Fargo. They've been trying to find a buyer for the past three years. I have it on good authority that the parcel will be going up for auction in another month or two.

"So, any goings-on there are off-the-books," she added, reading Tiff's mind.

Hazel lowered her voice to a whisper.

"As for the next part... I may have broken a few guidelines in the AICPA code of conduct so I wouldn't take any of the following information as legal evidence. I made some inquiries regarding Weston. He owns one rather large home in the Chastain Park neighborhood. But there is another listed under his name. His parent's property reverted to him via power of attorney when his mother went into a nursing home. He does make a significant amount of donations to local charities, but it's all handled by his lawyers.

"You should look him up, he has an interesting backstory. But I see nothing that raises red flags. Or at least, he's not doing anything shady in terms of the IRS. I also peeked at your PI databases. Aside from a DUI, he doesn't have any other legal or criminal issues." Hazel pushed the two pieces of paper across the desk and winked. "Shred those when you're done."

Tiff took the papers and stared back at the woman. She found herself wondering if one of Hazel's previous employers were intelligence agencies.

"You've outdone yourself this time."

Hazel gave the fairy a sly smile. "Need anything else?"

"I don't think so. I was just about to look Weston up when you came in."

"Alright. I'll let you get back to it then. Let me know if you want to grab lunch next week."

Tiff stepped from behind her desk and hugged Hazel goodbye.

"Thanks as always. You're on for lunch next week, my treat."

Hazel let herself out and Tiff turned back to the search results on Charles Weston. The first link was a human-interest piece from a local news outlet. It showed a picture of a much thinner and younger Charles in the iconic apron and chef's hat cutting a ribbon outside of his first establishment.

Tiff shook her head and looked away from the computer monitor briefly. The minute Stacey recognized his ID picture something felt off. While he wasn't a celebrity, Charles Weston was a recognizable face around town. He had a lot to lose by getting involved in human trafficking and not much to gain.

She turned back and skimmed over the article. Weston was a rags to riches type of story. He was an Atlanta native who put himself through culinary school. However, on the opening night of his fourth restaurant, his story took a grim turn. After too many drinks, Weston got behind the wheel of his brand-new BMW and wrapped it around a tree.

Ambulances rushed Weston to the hospital where he was diagnosed with a skull fracture, internal bleeding, and several vertebral compression fractures. His condition was further compounded after doctors discovered signs of stage 3 bone cancer. Luckily, he avoided suffering any spinal cord injuries. Between surgery, occupational therapy, and chemo, he had a long and grueling road to recovery ahead of him.

Then the miracle came. An hour before his scheduled surgery, Charles baffled doctors by getting to his feet and walking away. While he was still covered in extensive bruising, X-rays showed no signs of any broken bones. Blood tests confirmed he still had the cancer, but all things considered, his bones appeared healthy. Charles claimed to have no memory of the event at all.

"Ahh..." Tiff said aloud.

Things were getting clearer. She thought back to Dawn's comment about the catered breakfasts at the abandoned motel. The food was coming from Weston—or his restaurants at least. The chef was a victim of sorts too. Not in the literal sense, but regarding his health. Jeck gave him back the gift of life. And she was certain he'd explained he also had the power to take it back. It was the perfect extortion scheme.

Aside from the drinking and driving bit, the article cast the man in a positive light. Tiff scrolled back up to the top of the article. It was dated before Mallory's initial disappearance. That backed up her theory. She hit the browser's back button and looked for other articles written on Charles Weston.

The media loved gossip, and yet there was no mention of an arrest six months ago. She was there when officers cuffed Weston, Jeck, and a third man and then shoved them into squad cars.

Her eyes grew wide as she thought about the ramifications of Jeck's medical intervention. If he helped Weston, it was likely he'd done the same for countless others. Jeck could have an army of individuals indebted to him. Not just that, he was also solidifying his anchor along the way. Since Charles was kept out of jail, some of those connections were likely high up. Theoretically, anyone could be part of Jeck's network: the police chief, the mayor, only the gods knew who else. She scratched her head and worked through the possibilities.

The partially constructed condo development where Mallory and Kate were held six months ago was another good example. To use the space, Jeck would need to halt construction for a few days. With a foreman or a city inspector in his pocket, that was easy to obtain.

Her head started to hurt. She could probably spend countless hours gathering a list of places with authorized building permits where construction was suspended. Hazel gave her a list of Weston's properties and restaurants, but she wasn't sure visiting them would do any good. Even if the man was a puppet, his eateries were public places.

Tiff's stomach let out a loud gurgle that disrupted her train of thought. She reached beneath the desk and pulled open the door of the mini fridge. All that was inside was bottles of water. That was no good. She needed sugar.

The fairy checked the clock. It was almost 1:30 PM. By the time she grabbed something from the lobby and gathered her things, she could meet up with Mallory's friend. At least it would take her away from the research for a while.

She locked up and jogged down the two flights of stairs to the main floor. The convenience store near the corner of the lobby was empty. Tiff strolled past the racks of snacks and grabbed a handful of packages of Swedish Fish without slowing down. From the open refrigerated section, she grabbed a prepackaged turkey sub and a 20 oz. Dr. Pepper.

Tiffemory set the items on the counter and craned her neck around the counter looking for someone to ring her up.

"Sorry," said the woman sitting in the corner on a stool leaning against the wall. She shoved her cellphone into her pocket and walked over to the register. The girl looked back and forth between Tiff and the pile of junk food on the counter.

"Lunch," Tiff said with a smile.

"You must have one hell of a sweet tooth... And a fast metabolism."

"Guilty. I can't get this stuff back home."

After paying for the goods, Tiff headed back upstairs. From the end of the hall, she noticed a man standing in front of her door. Mallory's father turned toward her when she approached.

Craig Sanderson was a clean-shaven man in his mid-forties that stood a few inches shorter than six feet. She wasn't sure he owned anything more than suits and slacks as she'd never seen him in anything else. Today his outfit was all black, matching his hair, aside from a lilac-colored dress shirt.

"I like the shirt. It's a nice change to the boring white I always see you in." She pointed to his chin. "The facial hair suits you too."

He smirked and straightened his collar. "This was a Christmas gift from Mallory. She said it would help me stand out. Sorry for showing up unannounced."

"I just ran downstairs to grab something to eat," she said, lifting her purchases. "Come on in."

Craig moved out of the way so she could open the door and then walked in behind her. Tiff set her sandwich and snacks down on the desk and took a seat.

"Don't let me stop you," he said, grabbing one of the two chairs across from her. "It's late and you're probably starving."

Tiff took the plastic wrap off the sub, wadded the tomatoes in it, and tossed the bundle into the trash. She dumped two bags of Swedish Fish between the bread and lettuce followed by several packets of sugar. When she was satisfied, she alternated bites of the sandwich and swigs of soda.

Craig scrunched up his face as he watched. "Stacey would lose her mind seeing you eat that."

Tiff smiled and tossed an escaped gummy fish back into her mouth.

Craig leaned forward and cocked his head to the side to catch a glimpse of the documents from Hazel. He sat back again when Tiffemory snatched the papers and slid them beneath her laptop.

"Stacey told me you asked about the alarm system," Craig said, straightening his suit coat. "Mallory disabled it last night and then enabled it again shortly after. It looks like you were right about her sneaking out.

"What did you find out? Give it to me straight."

Tiff wiped her mouth and set the sandwich down.

"I'm sure Stacey also told you I'm to blame for all of this." Tiff ran her tongue over the raw patch of skin on her lip. "I know who's taken your daughter. It's the same person who took her last time."

"Why?"

"He's looking to settle a score."

"You never seemed surprised that he escaped from jail."

Craig's eyes narrowed when Tiff didn't respond.

"You know who he is, don't you? And I presume he's dangerous."

"I do. And he is. Mallory shouldn't be in any danger though. He's using her to get to me. Before I took him down last time, he offered me compensation in exchange for looking the other way."

"And how does Charles Weston play into her kidnapping?"

"I can't go into too much detail, but he's a victim in all of this too." While she couldn't tell him the whole truth, she at least felt more confident being able to tell him a portion of it.

"So, he wasn't involved in Mallory's abduction?"

"I don't have anything to confirm that presently."

Craig put his forearms on the desk and leaned closer. He raised the volume of his voice.

"Is this the same Charles Weston that owns Weston's Steakhouse? The place where she was taken from six months ago?"

"Yes," she said, keeping her voice calm. "But there's no evidence showing he's involved. I've looked through all my prior cases. Nobody else has gone missing from any of his other properties. I am still looking into him though. If I find anything, I will take action."

Craig nodded, finally satisfied enough to drop it.

"Do you mind if I look at the other picture you showed Stacey? I know I'm not in Atlanta much, but I'd like to see it nonetheless."

"Of course." Tiff handed over the folded page and then took another bite of her Swedish turkey club.

Craig flattened out the sheet of paper and studied it intently. After snapping a picture with his phone, he carefully folded it along the existing creases. He dropped it onto the desk and then did a double-take.

"Were you able to get through to her cell?" he asked, tapping the number jotted on the back of the paper.

"What?"

"That's Mallory's cell number. Didn't you get that from Stacey?"

Tiffemory picked the folded square up and then dug the sheet of paper from Craig's ex. She held the two side by side. They were a match. She shook her head.

"No. It came from a police officer. This man went to the precinct and was inquiring about me. And before you ask, now I'm sure this man is involved."

Tiff cursed herself for overlooking the number. If she would have made the call from her cell phone instead of her office phone, she would have made the connection. She decided to save him the details of the first time she called.

"The couple of times that I tried this number, I only got her voicemail."

"I know. I've tried calling her too." Craig took a deep breath. "Her voicemail is full now."

"Did you give Mallory's number to the police? Maybe they could find it."

Craig nodded.

"And have they found anything yet?"

"No. They mentioned her phone has been off since last night. What else can I do?"

"Nothing right now. My next step is to talk with Julie. Hopefully, I can finally piece together a few more leads."

When Craig was silent for a while, she resumed eating her sandwich. She watched him watch her eat and wondered what was going through his mind. Aside from raising his voice when he suspected she was holding back details about Weston, he remained unbelievably calm. The last time he sat in her office explaining how his daughter had disappeared he was an absolute mess.

"Why haven't you used the tooth yet?" Craig asked when the sandwich disappeared from her fingers.

Tiff stopped mid-chew. Goosebumps marched up her arms and down her neck, meeting somewhere in the middle. She resumed chewing, but a little too late. Craig noticed her hesitation.

"That's how you find all these missing people, isn't it? I've talked to some of your other clients. On every occasion, you required a tooth from them."

Tiff raised an eyebrow. "How'd you get access to my client list?"

"Everything you put in your phone syncs to your laptop..."

She interrupted him with a loud sigh. "Which you have some way of getting remote access to I presume."

Craig folded his arms across his chest. "How do you do it? Some kind of Voodoo?"

"Does it matter? It's one of the costs for my help."

He looked deep into her eyes, desperately searching for something to satisfy his curiosity. Fortunately, he backed down first.

"I suppose not," Craig said softly. He stood up and pushed the chair aside. "I'll let you get back to it. Thanks Tiff."

"I'll call as soon as I know something."

After Craig left, she looked down at the folded piece of paper and thought about what Craig had done. As the chief security officer of a Fortune 500 defense contractor, he was in a powerful position. He probably had a good chance of getting the man identified if he happened to be on a watch list. While she didn't have as extensive contacts, it was worth a shot.

She unfolded the paper again and snapped a picture of the unknown man. After fumbling with her phone for several minutes, she managed to get the image sent to Joshua. His response came within a minute.

"I can't help you with a name, but he was the one who ordered his goon to rough me up."

Damn. Her hunch was right. It was impossible to cause that amount of damage to someone from a simple flurry of blows. Even though he never touched Joshua, the unidentified man in the corner was behind his fracture.

That meant she was facing off against two fairies. Things just kept getting better.

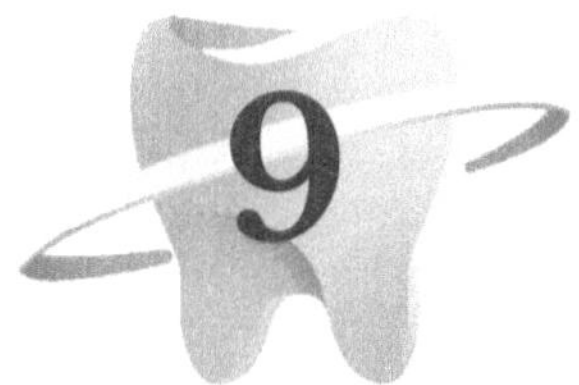

Tiff stood on Julie's front porch waiting for someone to answer the door. The girl agreed to meet but not until her father could be present. That meant waiting until 5:30 PM. If the custom license plate and decals adorning the red pickup in the driveway were accurate, Dad was a fireman and a staunch advocate of his second amendment rights. It was hard to blame the girl for being cautious. Especially considering her best friend's unfortunate knack for getting kidnapped.

The front door came open and out stepped a man who looked like a stereotypical lumberjack. Julie's dad didn't have any visible tattoos, but the full beard, sleeveless flannel, and accompanying scowl made him every bit as intimidating without them.

"Whaddaya want?" he said, crossing his arms over his chest.

"Tiffemory Greenstone," she said, holding out her investigator's license. "I'm looking into Mallory Sanderson's disappearance. May I come in and ask your daughter a few questions?"

The man snatched the card from her hand and examined it. He leaned his head out the door and looked up and down the street. When she passed his threat assessment, he stepped aside just enough to allow her to squeeze past him.

"Come on in."

Tiff stepped inside and was greeted by the smell of cooking meat.

"I didn't catch your name," she said looking up and offering her hand.

"Brett."

Julie's father squeezed her hand like a vise. Tiff returned the favor, digging her thumb into the back of his palm. Without needing to use a bit of her power, she ground her digit back and forth impinging his median nerve with his metacarpal bones.

Brett loosened his grip and let his hand fall back to his side.

"You're smaller than I expected, but every bit as badass as Mallory claimed." He walked over to the stairway to the second floor and yelled up. "Hey Cupcake, the detective's here."

Julie came down the stairs two at a time, somehow managing to avoid tripping over her baggy, pink pajama pants. Dark, frizzy curls framed the girl's round face. The glint of a diamond stud somehow detracted from a nose a tad too big for her face.

"Thanks, Dad."

"Why don't we all take a seat at the kitchen table," he said.

The trio moved toward the east end of the house. Tiff took the first open seat and Julie beside her at the head of the table. Brett stayed standing behind his daughter's chair—his arms across his chest, naturally.

"I was hoping I could talk with Julie alone."

"Anything you have to say to my daughter you can say in front of me."

"Let's be honest, teenage girls—hell any teenager—have plenty of things they'd find difficult to say in front of their parents."

"It's okay Dad, you can go," Julie said, leaning her head back.

"You're a minor and this is my house, so this is non-negotiable. And Julie, make sure you tell her everything she needs to know. I promise you that I won't be mad. You think I was an angel as a kid?"

"Okay, Dad."

The young girl turned back to face the fairy and tucked a lock of her brown hair with red highlights behind her ear.

"Is there a boy?" Tiff asked.

"Sort of. Mallory met someone online a few months ago but had never met him. His name's Johnny and he goes to Alpharetta High. He messaged her last night that he and a friend were sneaking out to go to a dance club. She agreed to finally meet up last night.

"So, we snuck out and went." Julie looked back at her father again. "I'm sorry, Dad. It was an under twenty-one place and there were no drugs or alcohol, I swear."

To Brett's credit, his facial expressions didn't change. He only gave a simple nod.

"Do you know Johnny's last name?"

"Yeah. It's Colins. With one L. He has several social media accounts. Mallory was careful."

"And the name of the club?"

"The Centrifuge, near Midtown."

Tiff scrawled some notes while Julie continued.

"Before we even got inside the club, a kid walked up to us with something the size of a jewelry box." She moved her hands, giving Tiff an idea of the dimensions. "He told us Johnny couldn't make it but sent it with his friends as an apology.

"Mallory politely declined but he said under no circumstances was he allowed to take no for an answer. He shoved the box into her hands and then sort of limped off. She was creeped out and we decided to leave immediately."

"Did you notice anyone following you?"

Julie chuckled.

"No. Mallory made sure of it. She drove to the police department parking lot and we sat there for fifteen minutes. There weren't any vehicles that pulled in behind us or waited at the side of the road. Nobody followed us."

"And you've never seen the kid before that approached you?"

The girl's curly mop bounced as she shook her head.

"Did you see what was in the box?"

"Yeah. We looked while waiting in the lot. It was an elaborately carved bracelet. There were no markings or receipts, but it looked expensive and made of ivory. She texted Johnny to tell him that she couldn't accept his gift. She wanted to give it back, but he never responded.

"When she dropped me off at home, I started going through all of Johnny's photos. The guy who handed her the box wasn't in any of them. I told her to text me when she got in. Five minutes later she messaged me—that's about how long it takes her to get home—so I presumed she was fine. Earlier this morning she messaged me and said she wasn't feeling well. I figured that's why she wasn't in school. She hasn't responded since."

The teen fought to hold back the tears. Her father knelt beside the chair and embraced her. She buried her face in his shoulder.

Aside from sneaking out of their houses, the girls did everything right. They realized something was wrong and left. But if Mallory took a trinket crafted from a fairy's bones her stalker wouldn't have to follow them. It would lead him directly to her over any distance.

Tiff wanted to scream. But that wouldn't get her any closer to finding Mallory. She reached out and touched Julie's hand.

"I need you to know neither of you is to blame because the two of you did everything right. You weren't being followed. The person who took Mallory was waiting at her house."

Tiff tapped her finger against the pen. There were plenty of questions to ask but she wanted to put the least amount of strain on Julie as possible. There was little point in showing her the picture of the other fairy. He and Jeck were using errand boys instead of risking being seen.

"There wasn't a bracelet for you too, was there?"

Julie sniffled and wiped her eyes.

"No. There was just one in the box. I'm not uhm… interested in boys. Would it help if I tried to describe the patterns on it?"

Tiff shook her head.

"No. I already know where it came from."

"Is there anything else you need, then?" asked Brett, rising to his feet.

"Just a couple more questions if you don't mind. I was hoping you could tell me what Mallory was wearing that night?"

"Yeah. She had on a brown, cold shoulder sweater and… Hang on. I took a selfie of the two of us. I can show you." Julie dug into her pocket and pulled out a smartphone. She held it close to her chest, punched in an unlock code, and discreetly swept her finger around the screen for a while.

"Here," she said, handing the phone over.

The screen showed the two girls sitting atop the hood of a blue car, presumably Mallory's from Stacey's description. Julie was to the right of center dressed in black jeans and a black top with lace sleeves. Mallory sat beside her; her left leg draped over Julie's. She had on the sweater Julie described and a pair of faded jeans.

Tiff pulled Dawn's fake ID cards from her purse and handed it to Julie along with her phone.

"Do you recognize this girl at all?"

She shook her head and gave it back. "No, is she missing too?"

"No. She's safe now." Tiff stood up and pushed the chair back in. "Thank you, Julie, and Brett. This was extremely helpful."

"Come on, I'll see you out," her father said.

He stepped forward and held the door open for her. Tiffemory handed him a business card and walked to her car.

"You're going to bring her back, right?" Julie called from behind her.

Tiff stopped on the sidewalk and turned to face the girl.

"Even if it kills me."

Tiff slid into the driver's seat and punched the dash. Her blonde hair fell to her shoulders as she removed the chopsticks holding the bun in place. As if sensing her tension, they transformed back into Gareth's original keepsake.

She closed her eyes and counted to five while taking deep breaths. Julie's side of the story didn't get her any closer to finding Mallory, but it filled in a few pieces and clarified the timeframe. And it gave her more of an idea about what type of a person Jeck was. He was an unscrupulous piece of trash willing to pervert their most intimate practices for self-gain.

While she hadn't learned much, Tiff called Craig and relayed everything. He was appreciative and promised to forward the information to the authorities.

She hung up and tossed the phone back in her purse. It struck the small shark tin with a metallic clang. She bit her lip and looked at the container. This was going to end tonight. First, she needed to grab a few things.

***

After Tiff wolfed down a microwave burrito, she reached under her bed and pulled out a sealed metal case the size of a shoebox. The two clasps came free, revealing a foam insert with three slots cut into it. Two black molded tubes flanked a blue glass bottle covered in warning stickers. She grabbed one of the tubes and squeezed the side. The plastic opened on its hinge revealing a filled syringe.

She raised the hypodermic needle to the light. The milky-white silver nitrate solution gave her a shiver. The one and only time she used the stuff was on Jeck. It worked like a charm. Despite being described as human mythology's cure-all to supernatural creatures, silver wasn't deadly to her kind. It did excel at nullifying their powers and eroding their anchors, though. She pressed the cover shut and dropped both into her purse.

Beneath the fitted foam insert was a pile of cash. Without bothering to count, she removed a handful of bills from her life savings. Unlike everyone around her, the money held no significance. It was simply there to keep her fed, her car fueled, and to cover the costs of anything she needed for cases. It's not like she planned on retiring here.

The only other things she needed were her Leatherman multi-tool and the chopsticks already in her hair. She placed Weston's wallet and the printed photo on top of the rest of her money, replaced the foam, and tucked the entire case back under the bed.

Her phone beeped, signaling the arrival of her rideshare. She locked up and approached the driver's side window of the silver Mitsubishi Outlander in the driveway.

The window rolled down and a young man in a tee-shirt, flannel, and ripped jeans poked his head out.

"I'm Marx, your driver. You're going to an address in Marietta, right?"

"That's only my first destination. I have multiple stops if you can accommodate my itinerary." Tiff held out a piece of paper. "Don't feel obligated though as I understand this isn't customary. But I'd be willing to compensate you well if you're available to drive me around all night."

The driver accepted the list and ducked his head back inside. He mumbled aloud while reading through the stops.

"A home in Marietta, a restaurant in Marietta, a condo development in Sandy Springs and then another in Roswell, through Alpharetta, and various spots throughout downtown." He turned to face the fairy again.

"What does '*through* Alpharetta' mean?"

"We may take some detours as I don't know what I'm looking for. But I'll know it when I see it." Tiff pulled a handful of twenties and fifties from her purse and fanned them out in front of the young man.

Marx scratched his head, checked the gas gauge, and then studied her face.

"You're not doing anything illegal, are you?"

She shook her head.

"Fine by me," he said, rubbing the back of his neck. "I guess?"

Tiff took a seat in the back and buckled her seatbelt.

"My name's Tiffemory, by the way."

They exchanged a handshake and Marx entered the address of Charles Weston's childhood home into his navigation system and then consulted the list again. He looked between Tiff and the list several times before speaking up.

"Did you want me to follow this list in order? We're not too far from some of these places right now. This has us zigzagging all over the place."

The house where Charles Weston grew up was her first destination. She wanted this to take priority and then the two commercial construction sites being managed by the same builder where Mallory was previously held.

Jeck knew how she tracked down Mallory the first time. If he wanted to keep the girl hidden, he'd have her stashed as far away as possible. Eight hours was a decent amount of time to find Mallory but still limited. It made sense to check the farthest destination first.

"The order is important, so I'd like you to follow it. Please."

"Is this part of a scavenger hunt or something?"

"Yeah. You could say it's something like that."

"Okay..." he said, shrugging his shoulders. "It's your dime."

Marx pulled onto the street and headed to the first destination.

"Are you a college student, Marx?"

"I'm in my junior year at Georgia Tech working toward a double major in mathematics and graphic design."

Tiff laughed. "Better you than me. I'm not particularly good at either of those things." She caught a glimpse of a smile in the rearview mirror.

"So, what do you do for a living, Tiff? That is if you don't mind me asking."

"I'm a private investigator."

"Oh. This is for a case then?"

"It is."

Marx let out a massive sigh of relief.

"I bet you thought I was a massive weirdo, huh?"

"I have to admit that the thought did cross my mind once or twice," he said. "So, a private eye, huh? Let me guess, you're on the trail of a cheating lover. I presume all of these restaurants are his favorite spots."

"No. I'm not that kind of detective. I deal solely with missing persons."

"Oh. Well, I'm sure that's more rewarding."

Tiff smiled. "More than you'd know."

After another twenty minutes of small talk, the car slowed to a crawl.

"We're at the first address, Miss. Did you want me to pull into the driveway? Will you be staying long?"

"No, the curb's fine. I'm not going to be getting out."

Marx watched in the rearview as Tiff shifted into the SUV's middle seat and affixed the lap belt around her waist. She pulled her legs onto the seat and sat cross-legged.

"Give me a minute and then you can head to the next destination. If you can avoid any sudden stops or potholes, I'd appreciate it."

Tiff unscrewed the lid of the tin from Stacey. The three pieces of Mallory's old tooth clung to one side. She tilted her head back and dumped the contents into her mouth.

The pieces reunited, melding together as they traveled down her esophagus. A discomfort rose in her throat from the lump, like heartburn. Tiff focused, directing her attention to the material so it didn't fully absorb into her system.

Her eyes snapped shut. The faint hum of the engine diminished until it was as silent as the wind. Gradually her vision returned, but not in the typical sense. The world reappeared in a muted tone like military night vision goggles, but gray instead of green. This was a different application of her power than she'd used at the airport. Instead of sensing an overlay of skeletal structures atop her vision, she felt her consciousness slip up and out of the car. Thousands of fuzzy outlines came into being within a 360-degree sphere around her. Some sat still, only moving periodically, some milled about, and others did... other things as they went about their everyday lives.

Tiff's stomach grew queasy. After a few minutes, it subsided and felt as natural as breathing.

This was something she couldn't accomplish while driving herself around. At least not if she wanted to avoid a fatal accident. Focusing her powers in this manner doubled her sensory range, extending it to a four or five-mile radius. Unfortunately, it was also more taxing on her anchor.

Marx turned around in his seat and faced the entranced fairy.

"Are you ready to move on now?"

She didn't respond.

Marx waved his hand inches from her face. He reached out to touch her shoulder and then thought better of it. His fingers punched the address of the second destination into the car's navigation system—Glacier Heart Cafe—and pulled away from the curb.

Tiff knew they were moving again when the thousands of indistinguishable people picked up speed and exited her viewing radius. Nobody stood out in sharp contrast and there was nobody she was drawn toward. Mallory wasn't anywhere near the house Weston inherited. Tiff's breathing slowed as she scanned the hundreds of new people entering the bounds of her senses every second.

Marx drove in silence for a while before turning the radio on to the Braves broadcast. He watched in the mirror, turning the volume up one notch at a time to ensure the noise didn't disturb his passenger. Tiff remained oblivious as the odometer ticked up. He dutifully stopped at each location and waited a minute or two, before checking it off the list and plotting a route to the next.

Tiff's body jostled about in the back seat without saying as much as a word while he escorted her around the greater Atlanta area. She was locked in a meditative state and not even aware of the car's seat beneath her. Neither time nor distance meant anything anymore. However, the one thing she *was* aware of was that the powers that be were taking notice. They homed in on the ongoing use of a power it knew didn't belong in Atlanta.

There was an itch that couldn't be scratched. It moved from her chest out to her extremities and back again. The fairy shrugged it off, letting her senses wash over thousands of additional people. This went on for a while until the itch was soon replaced by gentle pinching. Something pulled the fairy's skin in all different directions. The feeling wasn't painful but was unnerving.

She was going to have to stop sooner rather than later. This was the telltale sign of her anchor weakening. Tiffemory held out a little longer. Mallory was somewhere among the five million people in Atlanta.

And then the gentle tugs were overshadowed by an abrupt jerk.

The world spun and she snapped her eyes open. The interior of the car came into focus but there were hundreds of tiny blind spots. Her head wavered in circles as her visual cortex struggled to take over.

Tiff's legs shot to the floor. She reached out and clung to the headrest in front of her to steady herself.

Marx jumped in his seat.

"You're awake. You're not going to throw up, are you? Do you need me to pull over?"

She shook her head despite the taste of bile at the back of her throat. Stopping the car was out of the question. The tooth in her intestinal tract was tethered to something. A taut, invisible thread strung between her and Mallory. The girl was close. Somewhere toward the northwest.

Tiff's grip tightened on the bucket seats. She looked out the window. The headlights of the car were on, as were those of the dozens of other cars spread out on the five-lane highway.

"Where are we? What time is it?" she asked through parched lips.

"It's almost half-past nine. We left downtown about twenty minutes ago. I'm on the way to your last stop—Weston's Steakhouse."

The tether grew tauter and tauter as the SUV cruised down the expressway. They passed under a large green sign indicating the exit for Truist Park a mile ahead.

"Is there a home game tonight?" she asked.

Marx blinked absently at her reflection in the mirror.

"Yeah... I can turn it up if you can't hear the game. They're ahead—five to three in the bottom of the sixth."

Tiff shook her head—more so to make sense of things instead of answering the young man. Weston's Steakhouse was a part of the entertainment district outside Truist Park known as The Battery. The sprawling exterior mall complete with dining, shopping, and nightlife served as the perfect place to tailgate before a Braves home game. And apparently, an adequate kidnapping scene.

With a ball game going on at the stadium, The Battery would be busier than normal. Provided Mallory wasn't drugged as Dawn had been, there was no way to control a kidnapped victim in a crowded establishment. Unless the restaurant had a dungeon hidden beneath it. Tiff crossed her fingers and prayed that wasn't the case. When the vehicle started descending the exit ramp toward the restaurant, she realized something was wrong.

"Weston's Steakhouse is a few blocks ahead."

"That's not where we're heading anymore."

"Okay..."

"Keep going straight."

Marx turned onto Battery Avenue and slowed down. The car in front of him pulled over and unloaded a group of people, blocking their car in. Tiffemory leaned forward and tapped on the front seat.

The connection to Mallory grew stronger, pulling harder against her chest. The tether was strong enough to where she could imagine it. The invisible thread tugged at the tooth in her gut at a gentle upward angle. Tiff scanned the horizon and slapped her palm into her forehead.

This should have been the first stop on the list. Mallory was being held at the same condo development from her previous kidnapping.

She pointed at the structure towering beyond the ballpark.

"That's where we're going."

The twelve-story apartment complex was unrecognizable from the last time she was here. Instead of a windowless concrete shell, it was a work of art. Angular balconies jutted out from the gray and red facade. Marx pulled the SUV into the circular drive beyond a parkway full of flowers and a massive piece of marble with 'Zephyr Arms' chiseled into a massive piece of marble.

"Thanks," Tiff said, handing over the bills she'd shown him earlier. "Does this cover it?"

"That's more than generous."

The fairy grabbed her purse and strutted toward the glass double doors. Before she got too far away from the car Marx lowered the passenger window and called after her.

"Do you want me to wait for you?"

Tiff stopped. She had to fight to turn her back against the pull of Mallory.

"I don't know how long I'll be. I'll probably get a ride back with law enforcement."

Marx's eyebrows rose.

"What are you doing here?"

"Rescuing a kidnapped girl, if all goes well."

"Badass," Marx whispered. He blushed; unaware he'd been speaking aloud. "Good luck, I guess."

"Thanks," Tiff said with a smile.

Tiff didn't need the connection to Mallory to know exactly where to go. The third floor, near the middle of the building. That was where Mallory was tied to one of the building's support columns. She paused briefly at the entrance to the lobby. The door had an electronic key reader. Relief set in when she noticed the door still had a traditional tumbler lock. She slipped one of her chopsticks into the lock and it opened for her.

She went directly to the stairwell at the southwest corner of the lobby and made her way up. The third floor consisted of a long hallway that broke off into several offshoots. She passed by several doors until she came to one with a wreath of artificial black roses.

The pull from behind the door was overwhelming. To prevent it from clouding her senses, Tiff severed the connection. The tooth dissolved in her belly and its nutrients mixed in with the remnants of the night's hasty meal. All was still. The general tugging sensation was gone too. Her anchor seemed intact, but it was difficult to say to what extent. None of this was an exact science.

Tiff pressed her ear against the door.

The announcer of the Braves game could be heard over a television or radio. She reached out with her other senses. Mallory was the only occupant inside. She appeared to be propped up against the wall—probably gagged and restrained to the headboard of a bed. While her power provided no way of ascertaining someone's overall health, something felt off.

Tiff conducted a sweep of the surrounding units. Best she could tell, the few populated rooms held people going about their everyday activities. There was nobody crouched behind doors ready to ambush her and, more importantly, no strong glow from the bones of another tooth fairy. She directed her attention back to Mallory and did a more thorough inspection.

She couldn't put a finger on it, but something about Mallory's bones nagged her. Tiff clenched her fist and ground her teeth. Hopefully, Jeck and the other fairy weren't torturing her for information about her whereabouts. If the tooth led her here, Mallory was alive and inside the apartment. She had to move swiftly. There was no way to tell when her captors may be back.

The door clicked open under the fairy's makeshift lock pick. With her Leatherman multi-tool in hand, Tiff rushed inside. Aside from the hallway, the only light in the room came from the blinking 12:00 on the microwave and oven. Once her eyes adjusted to the dark, she noticed the condo was completely unfurnished.

An ad for an erectile dysfunction pill blared through the closed door ahead of her as she passed the bathroom. A faint light showed around the carpet fibers beneath the door where the noise came from. Tiff turned the knob of the door and flung it open.

"Let's get you out of here..."

Instead of Mallory, Tiff found Charles Weston on the floor. The man was propped up against the wall with pillows wedged behind his neck and under his knees.

The overweight man jerked up and cried out in pain. He thrust one hand out to steady himself but only succeeded in knocking over the compact radio sitting beside him.

"What the hell..." Tiff rubbed her eyes in disbelief. Her hands came away from her face too late to see the barrel of the pistol.

An explosion of light and sound drowned out the radio. Fire engulfed Tiff's shoulder. She dove backward out of the room as the gun barked again. A tiny section of the door frame splintered; exactly where her head had been.

Technically, this was Weston's third strike. But as much as Tiff wanted to make good on her previous threats, her powers were better suited when she had the drop on someone. By the time Weston got up from the floor and into the doorway, she'd have precious little time to target him. She was better off booking it.

The fairy retreated the way she'd come, snagging a tan, canvas jacket she'd missed from a hook on the back of the door. Heavy footfalls echoed down the corridor as she sprinted away. Tiff prayed the pain in his face meant she'd reach the stairwell before he could fire off more rounds. She breathed a sigh of relief as the heavy fire door slammed shut behind her.

Tiff probed the back of her shoulder while scurrying down the stairs. It hurt like hell, but she couldn't locate an exit wound. She wasn't sure whether that was a good or bad thing. Hell, she didn't know if the burning sensation was normal either. In the course of her job duties, she'd been hit, strangled, and stabbed, but never shot. She wrapped the jacket around her arm and held it in place.

The burning steadily grew in intensity and she became woozy. Tiff leaned against the railing and lifted the jacket enough to check the wound. A modicum of relief set in when blood didn't gush everywhere—at least it wasn't an arterial bleed. And then the vibrating sensation hit her.

She pulled down on the collar of her shirt and noticed a deep purple bruise already settling around the bullet hole. Small, discolored tendrils spread up to her collar and a few inches down her arm.

"Crap."

Not only had she been shot, but the bullet lodged in her shoulder was silver.

The fairy clutched the jacket to her shoulder harder and took the stairs two at a time. Despite the gravity of the situation, there was no time to deal with the wound now. Even if Weston wasn't giving chase didn't mean he still wouldn't. And there could be other assailants in the building.

The stairwell door burst open with a dull thud as it hit the cushion on the wall behind it. A pair of kids playing cards and a man reading a book turned to stare. Tiff walked backward to the main entrance, watching the three individuals carefully. None of them budged. All she was doing was drawing additional attention.

The Battery was the closest public space but was a mile away. There was a hotel and another apartment complex in the opposite direction. Both were equally far away. Finding somewhere to hide was her best bet. Her eyes settled on the highway onramp they passed when Marx dropped her off. It was only a few blocks away and would offer a small amount of cover. Hopefully, she could extract the bullet and have enough juice in the tank to fight if her pursuer found her.

Tiffemory made a mad dash, trampling through the flowerbed within the circular drive. A pair of headlights came to life, blinding her momentarily. She skidded to a stop and turned directions. Until she got the silver out of her body, running was her only chance. The fairy pumped her legs as hard as possible, putting the huge slab of marble between her and the car. The vehicle's engine started up. She shut her eyes, expecting to be run down at any second.

"Tiff!"

The fairy slowed and turned around at the familiar voice. Marx pulled the vehicle up alongside her.

"I figured there was no harm in sticking around. Your client wasn't here?"

"No," she said, watching the building behind them. "Does your offer to drive me home still stand?"

"Yeah... Holy shit, you're bleeding!"

Tiff frowned and looked down at the spreading red stain seeping through the canvas jacket.

"You noticed that, huh?"

Marx looked past her at the doors into the building. He nodded his head toward the car.

"Hurry, get in."

Tiff didn't wait to be told a second time. She scrambled into the passenger seat and slammed the door. He peeled out of the circular drive. The pair of them kept a constant watch on the rearview mirror, ensuring they weren't being followed.

When she was certain they were in the clear, Tiff peeled the jacket away from her arm again. The purple bruising was getting worse. She knew it was pointless but tried anyway. The fairy closed her eyes and focused on extending a tendril of bone from her scapula to search for the projectile. Once she could find it, she could force it out. Her entire arm felt like it was in a paint shaker without actually moving. Her bones didn't respond.

She pulled the chopsticks from her bun and tried manipulating them as well. The piece of bone undulated briefly but refused to form into the pair of slender tweezers she envisioned. It was going to have to come out by hand. As bad as the situation was, it brought a certain kind of satisfaction knowing Jeck went through the same thing when she injected silver nitrate into his thigh.

Tiff dug the multi-tool from her purse and folded the handles back. Her hands shook too badly to insert the pliers into the wound. Tiff screamed out, more in frustration than pain—though both were in ample supply.

The young man in the driver's seat looked over at her. "Are you crazy? Keep pressure on it until I get you to the hospital."

She reached up and turned on the dome light above their heads. "This can't wait."

Marx turned his head to peek at the wound. Purple lines snaked from her neck to elbow.

"What the hell did you get shot with?"

"Pull over," she shouted, ignoring his question. "We have to get the bullet out now. It's poisoning me."

"I chauffeur drunks around to make cash on the side. I'm not a doctor," he said, shaking his head. "We have to get you to the hospital."

Light-headedness set in. She worried for a moment that it was blood loss and then the sensation of hundreds of fishhooks tugging her in every direction set in.

"The bullet lodged in my shoulder is poisoning me. This can't wait for a hospital. We need to get this out now."

He locked eyes with her and saw the desperation in her face. The SUV's tires rumbled as it left the highway and slowed to a stop on the shoulder. Marx's shaking hands removed his lap belt.

"Okay... What do I do?"

Tiff handed over the heavy, stainless steel multi-tool.

"Like I said. We have to take out the bullet."

Marx looked between the pliers and the small bullet wound.

"You don't have any other smaller tools? These aren't going to fit."

Tiff tried once more to reshape Gareth's keepsake into something serviceable. This time the piece of bone didn't even wobble. She pulled her cell phone from her purse and used the flashlight to illuminate the operating area.

"I think this is all we've got."

As soon as Marx touched her skin with the pliers he pulled back. His face grew another shade paler, which Tiff didn't think possible.

"These aren't even sterile. And what if I pull on something I shouldn't?"

"It's okay. The thoracoacromial artery is several inches closer to my heart."

"The what? How do you know all this?"

"I read a lot." She wadded up the non-bloodied sleeve of the jacket and bit down on it. "And I would have already bled to death if it had. Please, just do it," she mumbled.

There was a squishing sound and a small spurt of blood as Marx pushed the tip of the pliers into the wound.

"Oh, God..."

Tiff bit harder and let out a cry as the skin tore around the metal implement.

"Wait. I feel something hard," Marx said after digging around for what felt like ages. "I think I got the bullet."

"Wait," Tiff cried out.

"Shit. Don't tell me that's your bone."

Tiff closed her eyes and fought through the pain to focus on her body. While she couldn't exert any control over them, she could still feel her skeletal structure. Whatever the pliers had clamped around wasn't bone.

"Do it," Tiff said. She shut her eyes and turned her head away from him. Hopefully, it wasn't something she needed.

Marx's hand moved steadily. Something glistened in the light of her phone and he gave it a quick tug. The bullet ripped free from her skin.

Marx held the bloody silver slug up to the light. "Holy crap. It's out!"

Tiff wrapped the jacket back around her shoulder and held it tight to the wound. It still hurt like hell, but the fishhooks diminished and the burning sensation subsided. It was subtle at first, but the purple streaks began to fade.

Marx held the pliers at arm's length while drips of blood fell into the cup holder in the center console. His eyes roamed the interior of the car, trying to determine what to do with the bloody implement.

"Here," Tiff said, holding open the jacket's breast pocket. After he dropped the silver bullet inside, she buttoned it up and wadded it back into a ball.

Loose gravel and dust flew up from the back tires as he pulled back onto the highway. "I'm taking you to the hospital." Mark sped up and neurotically changed lanes while checking the mirror more frequently than necessary.

"No hospital. Just keep driving while I think."

Tiff sank back into the seat, held the jacket tight, and tried to relax as much as someone who'd just been shot could. If someone else was after her, the ambush would have come during their impromptu roadside surgery.

"You've been shot and poisoned, but you don't want to go to the hospital? What the hell are you wrapped up in?" Marx checked the rearview after every other word.

"It's complicated, to say the least. But you're not in any trouble." She licked her lips. "Can you be quiet so I can make a call?"

Marx shook a bit but nodded. "O-Okay."

Tiff wiped her Leatherman and bloody hands on the jacket and then pulled out her phone. She dialed the number for Jasper's precinct. A desk officer answered.

"Atlanta Police department, this is Sargent Butcher. How can I direct your call?"

"Can you connect me to Officer Cooper, please?"

"Can you please hold?" A minute or so later the man came back on the line. "I'm sorry, but Officer Cooper's not on duty tonight. Would you like me to forward you to his desk phone so you can leave a message?"

"Please."

"Just a moment."

"Hey Jasper, it's Tiff," she said after his recorded voicemail greeting gave its spiel. "I was following a lead on a missing person tonight and I thought I'd found her—unit 322 at the Zephyr Arms. When I went to check it out I... uh... sort of got shot. I wanted to run some things past you. If you could return my call as soon as possible, I'd appreciate it. Thanks."

Tiff hung up and placed the blood smudged phone back into her purse.

"Hospital now?"

Not only did she not have health insurance—something that was sadly a prerequisite for getting someone to care about your wellbeing—but they would start asking questions about how she got shot. She had to hope that Joshua's crew could provide an alternative.

The fairy shook her head. "A little girl's life is still at stake. Take me to The Derelict instead."

"I'm not familiar with the place. What is it?"

Tiffemory smirked. "A seedy bar near the Oakland neighborhood."

Marx shrugged. The movement caused a bead of sweat to drip down his brow and he reached up to wipe it away.

"I suppose a drink wouldn't hurt."

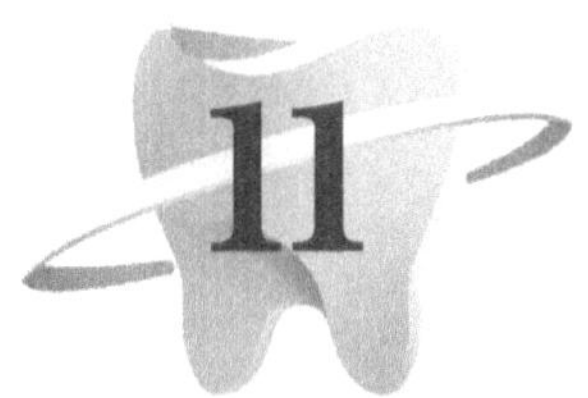

Tiffemory had no problem walking on her own but Marx insisted on keeping his arm around her in a pseudo-protective gesture. With the silver out of her shoulder, she was more than capable of defending herself but allowed the chivalrous act.

Once they stepped inside the bar, it was a different story. Marx stopped like a deer in headlights and made himself small. Slipping away from his arm, Tiff went on without him. He hurried to catch up after a trio of reserve soldiers dressed in fatigues turned to stare.

The Derelict was hopping compared to the previous night. Half of the dozen picnic bench tables were occupied along with most of the bar stools. None of them were as intimidating as Harley and Mark's group, but an air of welcome was still missing.

Tiff scanned the establishment on the lookout for Joshua. Neither he nor his retinue was present.

Marx turned to ask what they were doing there but shut his mouth when the big bartender approached. Cary, dressed in a similar gray button-up work shirt to the other night, stopped at their end of the bar. He narrowed his eyes, somehow aware of the dark blood spots on the jacket in the dim bar.

"What makes you think I need this kind of trouble in my bar, Shirley?"

Tiff bit her lip and looked down at her shoulder.

"I usually tend to my own wounds, but this is out of my wheelhouse. And I think you know that I can't exactly go to the hospital. I wasn't sure where else to go."

"I'm sure they wouldn't hold the fairy thing against you."

Tiff shifted her weight to the other leg. She hadn't realized the bartender knew her secret. A glance at Marx out of her periphery showed no reaction on his part. Either he hadn't heard the comment or was still in shock.

Cary closed his eyes and let out an exaggerated sigh.

"Go take a seat in the back and I'll stitch you up in a minute." He pointed a thumb past the end of the bar. "Lucy, I need you to keep an eye on things."

One of the bartenders, a gorgeous onyx-haired woman, smiled and nodded.

Marx looked to Tiff for validation, who shrugged her shoulders and headed toward a black tapestry hanging on the wall depicting two top hat-wearing skeletons flanking a Ouija board. As they wandered closer, she realized it was a novelty shower curtain blocking off a small hallway.

They pushed past the flimsy barrier and entered a corridor illuminated only by faint guide lights near the floor. Bottles jostled as she bumped into stacked crates of booze. She waited a moment for her eyes to adjust and then headed toward a glowing emergency exit sign. To their right was the metal door of a walk-in cooler. In a small alcove to the left was a U-shaped booth with a wobbly, circular table.

Tiff squeezed into the booth. Marx opted to stand so he could pace up and down the small hallway and chew his cuticles. He practically jumped when the curtain pulled aside again, and Cary walked back.

As Cary approached Tiff noticed a pistol holstered along with an extra magazine pouch on his hip. Marx was too busy staring at the woman following behind the bar owner. Lucy stood damn near six feet tall in heels. He glanced away and blushed when she caught him staring at the way her curves filled out her slashed black jeans and black and red corset.

Lucy set three glasses onto the metal table. A kiddie cocktail in a tall glass destined for Tiff, an old-fashioned glass with dark liquor, and a glass of water without ice.

"Thanks, Lucy," Cary said with a nod.

Marx watched her hips sway as she retreated to the bar floor. He picked up the smaller glass, smelled the amber liquid, and then took a swig.

"That was to disinfect my tools, ace," Cary said, setting down a tan medical bag and a red bar towel. He took the glass back from the driver and slammed it down on the table. Light bathed over the table as he pulled the chain of a single incandescent bulb hanging from the ceiling.

"Alright, let's see what we're dealing with."

The fairy cried out in pain as he grabbed her shoulder with his massive hands and prodded the wound.

"Small-caliber bullet wound. Who'd you piss off?"

The fairy grinned and he took a seat.

"The swelling is minimal, so it doesn't look like there is any sign of internal bleeding. You got lucky and the shooter didn't hit anything vital. Contrary to popular belief, twenty-two rounds are plenty lethal."

Tiff cringed as he wrenched her arm in the air and took a good look.

"What concerns me is that I don't see an exit wound..."

"We already removed the bullet," piped up Marx.

"I can see that. Using an excavator, from the looks of it. Probably not the best idea, but what's done is done." Cary didn't bother to turn and look at the young man. "Your friend looks a little green. How many times did he pass out while digging the bullet out?"

"He came through when I needed him."

"If you say so. Do you still have the bullet?"

Tiff unsnapped the breast pocket of the jacket taken from the condo unit and gave it a shake. The bloody bullet dropped onto the table with a clink.

Using a pair of forceps from his bag, Cary picked it up and held it up to the light. He looked back to her and then inspected the bullet more carefully.

"This is silver. Silver's less dense than lead, but it's also less malleable, which means it's less likely to fragment upon impact. Especially when the cartridge is packed with a reduced powder load. Whoever made this knew what they were doing."

"I'm not sure I understood all of that."

"The bullet was specifically made so it would stay inside of you. Now I'm *really* interested in whoever you pissed off, Shirley."

She looked down at the small crater in her shoulder and winced. "It's a long story."

"Does silver work against your kind?" Cary moved the forceps near the fairy causing her to scramble away from him. He smiled and dropped it into the glass of whiskey Marx sipped out of. "Good to know."

She frowned and kept an eye on him as he moved closer.

"You can relax. But you'll need a few sutures." Cary pulled a curved needle and thread from the first aid kit and then doused them and his hands with an airline bottle of vodka. He held them up high and glanced over to Marx.

"Care to give me a hand here, chief?"

The rideshare driver pushed himself away from the section of wall he'd been leaning against and stepped to the side of the table, emboldened by Tiff's defense of him. He looked a little more confident than he did on the side of the highway.

"What do you want me to do?"

"There's a bottle of iodine in the bag. I need you to rinse out the wound."

"You're going to do this here?" Marx said, looking at the unstable metal table. "This isn't exactly sanitary."

Cary looked Marx dead in the eyes.

"I'm more concerned about the health inspector dropping in. Look, kid, I served two tours in Afghanistan as a combat medic for the US Army. Now, kindly disinfect the wound and then get out of my way?"

Marx did as Cary instructed and then retreated to the safety of the wall again.

"You don't want something stronger than sugar water before we get started?"

The fairy shook her head and took a long swig of her drink.

"Suit yourself. Try to sit still and relax if you can."

Within a couple of minutes, Cary had the wound sutured and neatly dressed. By some miracle, he managed to sew up her wound without getting a single drop of blood on himself. He looked down at his handiwork and smiled.

"How does it feel?" he asked while dipping a clean rag in the glass of water and wiping down her shoulder.

Tiffemory moved her left arm in circles. Each rotation brought a sharp pain.

"Like I got shot."

Cary smiled. "Good. That's exactly how you should feel. Need anything for the pain?"

"Why? Do you deal in black market pharmaceuticals too?"

The man shrugged.

"No. I'd rather not deal with the grogginess or whatever other side effects my body wouldn't be used to."

"As you wish. Try not to move it around too much." Cary turned toward Marx. "Change the bandages every few days and keep them clean and dry. If it starts bleeding excessively, oozing funny colors, or starts to smell rancid, you need to take her to the hospital. It wouldn't hurt to do some physical therapy too."

Not sure what else to do, the young man nodded at each item on the list.

"Sorry if I bled all over your car." Tiff pulled a business card out of her purse and handed it to Marx. "Let me know what the cleaning bill comes out to."

"It's okay."

"Thanks for your help, Marx. I'll be okay from here. I need some time to process everything that happened tonight."

"Uh... Okay."

Marx looked blankly around the dimly lit area and then shuffled out of the back hallway.

"Drive carefully," Cary called out as the curtain swished back in place behind the young man.

"Your associate's a little wet behind the ears." The bartender raised the whiskey to his mouth, spotted the bullet at the bottom of the glass, and set it back down with a frown. "How long have you been working together?"

Tiff shook her head. "Oh, we don't work together. I just met him tonight. He was my Uber driver."

Cary laughed. "Chances are pretty good that he never picks up another passenger after tonight."

"You're probably right."

A thin shaft of light stretched out on the wall as the curtain pulled apart briefly again.

"Funny running into you here..."

Tiff looked up to see Joshua coming down the hallway with the aid of only a single crutch. A plastic bag hung from the fingers of his right hand. He wore a Hawaiian shirt patterned with little pineapples and ham shanks. Paired with open-toed sandals and navy-blue track pants, he looked... Comfortable.

"What are you?" Tiff turned and pointed her finger at Cary. "You called him. Ah, I get it. You're one of his partners. That's how you knew I was a fairy."

"Colleagues," Cary said, clearing his throat. "I'll give you two some privacy." The big bartender stood and scooped up his things. He held the glass of whiskey out toward her. "Some servicemen hang on to the bullets they're shot with as a good luck charm. Do you want to make a necklace out of it or something?"

"Hell no."

"I'll get rid of it for you then."

"Do you want to toss the rest of the evidence while you're at it?" Tiff joked, lifting the bloodied jacket.

"I suppose I may as well."

Cary walked off with his bag and the bloodied jacket tossed over one shoulder.

Joshua tossed his plastic bag in front of Tiff and sat down. Inside was a black fabric sling, a roll of cloth tape, and a box of gauze pads. She fished the sling out and struggled to fit her arm inside the device.

"Want me to..."

"Nah, I'm going to have to learn to do this myself anyway."

Joshua worked to balance his crutch against the wall as Lucy appeared with a draft beer. He took it directly from her and raised it to his lips.

"Lucy, right?" Tiff said before the woman could walk away.

"Short for Lucifer." The woman said with a wink. She pointed the blood-red fingernail of her pointer finger to the tattoo of a naked, devil girl complete with black wings and trident nestled just above her cleavage.

"I could use something to eat. What's good in the kitchen?"

"Yeah... We don't have a kitchen per se. Most people just come here to drink. I'd be happy to order you something from the burger joint down the street though."

"A burger would be to die for. And a mess of sugar packets too. If they have them."

"Sure, hon," Lucy said with a nod.

Joshua took another swig of his beer.

"I take it things didn't go too well tonight?" he said.

"You could say that. Thanks for the medical supplies, by the way." Tiff took another drink of the sugary, red drink. "Mind if I pick your brain? There aren't many people in Atlanta who know what I am. I don't have anyone else to bounce ideas off."

He wiped a thin layer of foam from his upper lip and set the glass down. "Sure, I sort of owe you anyway."

"What do you know about fairies?"

"Less than you, I imagine." Joshua laughed. After seeing the frown on her face, he placed his chin in the webbing between his thumb and pointer finger for a while to think.

"When I was a child, my mother told me all kinds of stories about fairies. Dark stuff, like the original Grimm fairy tales.

"I don't remember the intricacies. But the gist of them all involved a fairy who kicked ass and took names. The stereotypical hero who tried to right wrongs and fight for the underdog—that kind of stuff. What did make an imprint was the way Mom told them. They were personal to her. Like she was there, or at least fondly remembering the person who handed the tales down to her.

"As I got older, I came to realize they were more than just stories. I came across a box of photos, diaries, and newspaper clippings about Grandpa. When I confronted Mom, she told me everything. He more or less did the same things you're doing. Helping people that other people couldn't. Someone helped him fit in here and that's why I do what I do.

Joshua fished around in the left pocket of his gaudy shirt and palmed something. He turned the object over in his hands.

"Before I left for college Mom gave me this," He pushed the item to the center of the table. When he withdrew his hand, a three-inch-long, white rose lay in the middle of the table. "It was a gift to her from Grandpa."

Tiff didn't need to touch the rose to know it was bone. And one crafted with such detail that it could only have come from one of her kind.

"Do you know what your grandfather was capable of?"

"He disappeared after my grandmother died—which was before I was born so I have no first-hand accounts. But based on Mom's stories I have some ideas. Wouldn't you know better than I would though?"

Tiff frowned. "I know what I can do... but..." The fairy opened her mouth a few times trying to coalesce thoughts into words. "There isn't much need to flex our powers in Fae. Sometimes what I find myself able to accomplish here is surprising."

"What exactly is bothering you?"

"Are you aware of how we received the 'tooth fairy' moniker?"

Joshua nodded and lifted the beer to his lips.

"I used a girl's tooth tonight to track her down. Only when I found her, it wasn't her."

He set the beer down untouched. "Sorry, I'm not following. What do you mean it wasn't her?"

She gave him a full rundown of everything: starting six months ago with the rogue fairy and ending with tonight's shooting.

"So instead of finding my client's daughter, I found one of Jeck's overweight minions with a bone structure matching Mallory's."

Joshua choked on a mouthful of beer. "Talk about bait and switch." He wiped his damp chin with the back of his hand. "How could you have gotten that wrong? I got the feeling the bonds you formed were unbreakable."

"It is. I mean, at least as far as I know. "

"I haven't had much time to sort it out yet. Having been shot, and running for my life, and all."

He nodded. "So, you're trying to determine how it was possible." Joshua put his head down, lifting it frequently to take pulls of his beer until the glass was empty. "Hmm..."

He was about to head to the bar for a refill when Lucy came back and set a serving tray down on the edge of the table. She placed another beer in front of Joshua. Turning to Tiff, she set down a paper fast food bag and a cylindrical, glass sugar dispenser. Joshua slipped Lucy a ten. She slipped the bill into her back pocket, gave him a peck on the cheek, and disappeared again.

Tiff took the top bun off her burger and threw the slice of tomato back into the paper bag. She upended the glass shaker. Sugar settled into the nooks and crannies of the patty, turning pockets of grease into a sweet slurry. When it had a thick layer, she replaced the bun and took a large bite.

Joshua shook his head and lifted his fresh beer. "Mom said that grandpa had a sweet tooth too. I take it tooth fairies are immune to diabetes?" He cocked his head to the side and lowered the beer again. "Maybe that's it. What if it's a familial thing?"

"What do you mean?"

"What if the guy and the girl were related? Could that have accounted for the false positive?"

"No. It has more to do with esotericism and not genetics."

Joshua shook his head briefly and shrugged.

"The microcosm is the macrocosm. It's a matter of trying the part back to the whole."

"Okay," he said absently. He attempted to take another sip but instead cocked his head to the opposite side and set the glass back down. "What if a part of Mallory *was* there and that's what you picked up on? If I were asked to counterfeit something complicated, the best chance of success would be to create a direct copy from the original. What if Jeck did the same thing?"

Tiffemory set the burger down and licked the sugar dripping from her fingertips. There were no instruction manuals for what her kind could or couldn't do. It seemed possible that Jeck could have manipulated Charles's bones to a facsimile of the girls. And she liked that explanation better than the only other possibility that came to mind—grafted portions of Mallory's bones to Weston's.

"I don't even know what that would do to a person. Jeck may be more of a monster than I previously thought," Tiff said thinking aloud.

"He's trafficking children, so..."

Tiff finished her burger as well as her drink.

"Can I ask you a few more questions?"

"If you think it'll help."

"You mentioned the other night that you kept tabs on Outsiders in the city."

"For anyone that I hook up with an ID anyway. I kind of feel like it's part of my responsibility. I presume you're asking whether Jeck has been on my radar?"

"Yeah. And the mystery fairy."

Joshua shook his head.

"I haven't come across anything calling attention to your rogue fairy friends. As you mentioned, he's probably blackmailing others into doing most of the dirty work." Joshua took another long drink of his beer. "Officially, you're the only fairy I know of in town. That isn't to say that there aren't any others, of course. Did you have a chance to check into my competition yet?"

"The other counterfeiter? No, but it's on my to-do list. Usually having the child's tooth makes most of this detective work unnecessary."

"If you apply the right pressure, I'm sure he'll point you in the right direction."

Tiff nodded. "In the morning, probably. As much as I hate to let another day pass with Mallory still out there, I don't have any more leads and I need the rest."

"I'll keep my ears open. I can give you a lift home anytime you're ready."

"Okay, let me settle my tab."

"You're good."

"What?"

"Since you're with me, your money's no good here."

"Oh... Thanks. In that case, I think I'm ready."

Joshua stood up from the table and left the half-full beer on the table.

She stopped by the bar on her way out and gave Cary her thanks as well. Tiff looked around the joint. The place no longer had an intimidating feel. It may not have been full of Outsiders, but everyone inside was an outcast of sorts. Although she looked out of place, nobody stared at her like she didn't belong. It didn't hurt that the bartender knew his way around a needle and thread and let her eat and drink for free either.

Tiff shut the door to her basement apartment. She dropped her bag on the nightstand and fell face first into her bed. There was an immediate groan of regret as pain reverberated through her bandaged shoulder.

She walked to the bathroom and pulled up one edge of the tape to peek beneath the bandage. Her skin was pale around the black stitching. They were still in place and there wasn't any sign of fresh bleeding. She pressed the tape back down and shut off the bathroom light before settling into the armchair near the door.

The mobile phone felt heavier than it had any right to. This moment was one she'd been dreading ever since leaving the condo development. She owed Craig a phone call.

Her finger hovered over his contact entry. Knowing she should call him and knowing what to say were two different things. She was no closer to finding Mallory than last they talked. The list of unanswered questions kept growing.

Stacey had implied she didn't have any more of Mallory's baby teeth. Even if she or Craig managed to find one, Tiff couldn't guarantee Jeck didn't have other decoys stashed throughout the city. Any of which would inevitably be waiting to shoot her again.

She crossed her fingers. Maybe the authorities had better luck. Or they at least had some lead she could piggyback on. Tiffemory licked her lips, took a deep breath, and pressed the call button.

"Thank God you found her," Craig said after the second ring.

"Craig..." Her voice was low and cracked. She hung her head and swallowed the lump in her throat. "I... Didn't find her."

"What? What do you mean? You had her tooth. I thought that's all you needed."

"I tried," she whispered.

The line fell quiet for a minute. Tiff second-guessed every choice she'd made. Maybe her instincts were right, and Mallory was in the room with Charles. What if she was tied up in the closet and she just left her there? Her anchor was weakened and could have thrown her senses off. Or perhaps Jeck had some kind of silver lining in the room to mask the girl.

Tiff cursed herself for running and not facing Weston. She should have stayed at the Zephyr Arms until she searched every apartment if she had to.

"I'm sorry," she said, interrupting Craig's shallow breathing. "Things got crazy after I was shot."

"You've been shot? Where?"

"My shoulder."

"No. What I mean is, where are you?"

"I'm at home now but a man shot me in a condo building near The Battery. I tracked Mallory there and ran into an ambush." She wanted to tell him more. How she didn't call the cops because she technically broke in. How they would have had a suspect in custody if she had.

"Are you okay?"

"Yeah, I should be fine."

"What about Mallory? Did you see her? Is she okay?"

"I'm not certain she was ever there."

"Do you have any other leads?"

"I do..." she said with hesitation. Tiff wanted to tell him that everything would be fine but was starting to lose faith. While she had no intention of giving up, she didn't know how her other leads would pan out. The number of cases she'd closed without having a tooth at her disposal was few and far between.

"I'll do everything in my power to find her," she said, lifting her chin. "What have the police found?"

"They questioned John Colins, the kid that you mentioned earlier. They found him in the hospital, but it's not what you'd think. Believe it or not, he's been recovering from a kidney transplant.

"He isn't the one who's been in communication with Mallory, not that he was in any shape to meet Mallory at a club the other night if he was. His social media account was hacked or copied. That was a dead lead.

"Other than that, they haven't come up with anything useful. They still haven't found her car."

"I found another missing girl recently. She was in the process of being moved out of state. Have they circulated Mallory's photo around the airport?"

"We gave them recent photos of her. I don't know specifically what they've done with them."

Tiff racked her mind trying to think of any questions she could ask that would help. She tried to walk back through the details of Julie's story. Somewhere between dropping off her best friend at home and her own house, Mallory was taken. The bone bracelet would have allowed Jeck to intercept her at any point.

A light bulb went on in her head. Stacey mentioned Mallory had sequestered herself inside the house for months. However, Julie mentioned she'd been talking to 'Johnny' for a while. While it seemed Jeck had been patient in putting his plan into motion, he could have made other attempts to kidnap her. Maybe it wasn't the first trinket he'd sent her. If she could locate another, she could use it to track down Jeck. In turn, it should lead her to Mallory. Or Jeck, whom she could beat Mallory's location out of.

"Did they find anything of note in her room?"

"Aside from chat logs on her laptop, no. There were no signs of a struggle and as I mentioned this morning, the alarm in the house was still armed. I don't think the police spent a lot of time searching through her things."

"Would you mind if I came by early in the morning to look around? It's possible they overlooked something or didn't know what to look for."

"Yeah, I think that would be alright. I'll let Stacey know that you're coming."

"I have some other leads to follow up on too. I'll find a way to get this son of a bitch and bring Mallory back."

Truth be told, other than holding out hope that Jeck left a piece of himself behind, she only had the other counterfeiter to lean on.

"Okay," Craig said. "We'll see you in the morning, then."

"We? You're staying at the house?"

He paused for a second. "Yeah, I am."

"Sorry, I didn't mean to overstep. You're not going to have a black eye when I show up, are you?"

Craig chuckled. "We're well past that point. Stacey and I have been talking a lot recently. There was even a brief discussion about me moving back in. Though, I presume that's contingent upon whether or not..."

"Craig, I keep my promises. I will get Mallory back."

The line went quiet again for a moment.

"Thank you for calling me and letting me know." After a brief pause, he added, "I hope your shoulder recovers quickly."

"Thanks. I'll let you know when I have something else."

Tiff hung up and traded her phone for her notepad. She tapped the pen against the page absentmindedly. Searching all of Weston's properties got her nowhere. He was almost certainly nothing but a patsy in this. However, it did uncover a potential new lead. Unless Weston had broken in, someone had to own the condo unit where she found him. And Hazel probably had access to that information.

It was also worth trying to dig up more information on Weston in general. Most importantly, determining how he managed to get out of jail without any charges the first time around. If a crooked official got him out it might be another way to access Jeck. Hopefully, Jasper could shed some light on that one. At least if he was still willing to help.

Next, she needed to comb through Mallory's room—something she should have done earlier. Unless she found something to point her in a different direction, her last stop would be the dry cleaners Joshua mentioned. And if interrogating the morally flexible counterfeiter yielded nothing? She had nothing.

The fairy went through her bedtime ritual. She devoured a handful of chocolate candies, washed her face, and then cut the rest of her blouse off. With some difficulty, she slipped into a spaghetti strap tank top that would be comfortable to sleep in as well as wear out tomorrow.

Tiff glanced at the bookshelf against the wall lined with medical periodicals, textbooks, and junk food. After a moment she reconsidered. Sleep seemed more important. She dragged the armchair with her one good appendage until it was alongside the nightstand. She jumped in and propped her feet up.

As soon as she got comfortable and shut her eyes, the phone rang. She let out a growl and twisted to reach her purse. Pain echoed down her arm and it took her longer to answer than she hoped.

The display on the phone's screen was blank.

"Hello?" She said with caution. After the night she'd had she half expected Jeck's mocking voice in response.

"How's my favorite patient?" Cary asked over the din of a crowded bar. "You're not overexerting yourself yet, are you?"

"Not yet," she said, a smile crossing her lips. "But tomorrow is a new day." Despite his stunt with the silver bullet, Cary was a likable enough character. And it had been a while since someone had been looking out for her wellbeing.

The bartender laughed. "Well, I guess I'd better follow up tomorrow night then. I still think it would be a good idea to check in with a physical therapist. I presume you haven't done that yet."

"No. The case I'm working on is dominating all of my free time."

In the silence that followed Tiff seriously entertained asking Cary for help. The thought of facing off against two fairies terrified her. It was unheard of for a fairy to use their powers against one another. Not to mention the fact her last attempt to use them against Jeck was unsuccessful. To make things worse, they had to know she'd be coming—especially in the wake of Charles' failed ambush.

She desperately wanted help from someone. Anyone. Whether it was Cary, Joshua's entire brute squad, or Jasper and the authorities. The problem was that they'd never fought an Outsider before. Ultimately, any of them would be a liability. Even with the gruff bartender's medical and combat experience, he was still human. Worrying about them would leave her vulnerable and unable to focus.

None of it mattered if she couldn't figure track down Jeck.

He finally broke the silence, as if he knew she needed help, but was too prideful to ask. "Alright. Have a good night, Shirley. Godspeed with your case. You're welcome to come back when you inevitably pop those stitches."

"Thanks," she said before ending the call.

Every few minutes she readjusted in the chair to find a position that didn't bother her shoulder. Her mind worked overtime searching for some angle she'd missed. There was nothing there. Hopefully, an investigation of Mallory's room would uncover something useful.

But finding Jeck was only the first part of the problem. After that, she had to figure out what to do with him. Pumping him full of silver would only go so far. Short of scrawling a message in his chest and hoping his elders found it when he was pulled back to Fae, he'd come back again. It took several months, but that's what happened last time. While not ideal, it would give her time to devise a more permanent solution.

After another hour alone with her thoughts, Tiffemory fell into a deep sleep. This time she wasn't interrupted by the nightmares of what happened to her family. Even so, the pieces of bone tucked in her hair bubbled. Liquid bone flowed free from her hair and dripped into a puddle in her lap. As she slept, the fairy statue rose and nestled itself into her arms.

Tiffemory awoke in the armchair and stretched the stiffness from her neck. The digital clock on the nightstand reported a little after six. After going to the bathroom and inspecting her sutures again, she pulled the notebook from her purse and double-checked the list from last night. There was plenty of time to get to Stacey's and make it to the dry cleaners before they opened at eight.

She felt bad calling Hazel this early in the morning, but she needed answers ASAP. Even if she didn't hear back for a few hours, enlisting the woman's expertise freed her up to do the fieldwork. Limiting the amount of downtime increased the odds of finding Mallory. The girl had been missing for more than twenty-four hours now and every minute counted.

After a few rings, Hazel muttered a groggy 'Hello'.

"Hey, Hazel, it's Tiff. Sorry to wake you."

"It's okay," she said after a long yawn. "How are you doing?"

Tiff decided to forgo mentioning the bullet wound. She'd find out soon enough in person.

"I'm good. And you?"

"I can't complain. Is your current case still giving you trouble?"

"Yeah. Do you have some time to help me out with another property record search?"

"Yeah, hang on one minute. Let me get up and find a pen." A few minutes later she said, "Okay, go ahead."

"I'm trying to track down the owner or lessee of a condo. Unit 322 of The Zephyr Arms."

"I presume you'd like to know what other properties are in that individual's name as well?"

"Mmhmm."

"Okay. Once I shower and get some coffee in me, I'll see what I can dig up for you."

"Thanks. You're a lifesaver."

"For you? Anytime. Be careful, Tiff."

Tiff made a checkmark in the notebook and then gave Craig a ring to let him know she was leaving. Not surprisingly, he answered almost immediately.

"Are you on your way?" There was an anxiousness in his voice, but no hint of the grogginess that Hazel's had.

"I'm about to walk out the door now. I'll see you in about twenty."

Tiff slung her purse over her good shoulder. It contained everything she'd gathered so far related to the case: Weston's wallet, the fake ID, and the printed picture of the mystery fairy. She made sure the two plastic syringe cases were in there as well.

On her way out the door, she grabbed the last two sleeves of chocolate Pop-Tarts from the box on the bookshelf. Attempting to hold her breakfast, as well as the steering wheel with one arm, proved a unique challenge, but she managed. Twenty minutes later she pulled up alongside Stacey's house in Roswell.

Craig jumped up from one of the padded rocking chairs on the wrap-around porch as soon as she pulled up. She lingered behind the car for a moment to wipe the crumbs from her shirt before heading up to the house. This was the first time Tiff saw him out of a suit. To be fair, he still had on a pair of tan slacks and a dress shirt. Though the latter wasn't fully buttoned and exposed a fair amount of gray chest hair, so it wasn't exactly business attire.

"I see you've been a little rough on the car," he said pointing at the front right bumper. A frown broke across his face. "And yourself."

She glanced at her shoulder. "There's no permanent damage. It'll heal"

Craig held the front door open and she stepped inside.

Stacey's bare feet made a little squeak against the wood floor as she slid to a stop in the entryway. She didn't look as put together as Craig. Worry lines streaked her face that Tiff hadn't noticed the first time around and her hair was flat and full of tangles. Old sweatpants and a baggy long-sleeved tee hid the strong body of an athlete that was on display before.

Stacey looked down at the floor and bit her lip. "If they shot at you, does that say anything about what they might do to Mallory?" She fought to keep her hands still.

Craig walked up and wrapped an arm around his ex-wife.

"We shouldn't speculate. Tiff is good at what she does. Let's just get out of her way."

The fairy glanced at Craig and then back at Stacey. "I presume you're aware that I don't have any good news for you at this time. Though rest assured that I have a few leads to follow. Some colleagues of mine are looking into things as well. I'm still hopeful that they'll point me to your daughter." As she spoke the phone rang and buzzed in her purse. "Excuse me."

Tiff turned her back and checked her phone's screen. The caller ID displayed 'City of Atlanta'; most likely Jasper responding to the message she'd left last night. She silenced the call and looked back up to her hosts.

"Is that one of them?" Stacey asked. She rose on the balls of her feet. "Feel free to step outside and take the call if you need to."

"No. It's okay. I just touched base with them. I'm not expecting to hear back just yet. My undivided attention is here right now."

Stacey looked up at Craig and then back to Tiff. She nodded.

"I'm sorry. I know this is difficult for both of you. I'll try to make my visit quick.

"Julie mentioned Mallory received a gift from an admirer. I think she had it with her at the time of her disappearance, but I'd like to see if she made it back here with it. It's also possible that other gifts may have been shipped to the house."

"She gets packages from Amazon occasionally," said Stacey. "We both do. I guess I might not have noticed if they were from an individual. Wait..." She took a step forward. "Why didn't you tell me this before? Or the police? Couldn't they use this information to track her kidnapper?"

"Stace," Craig said. "We have to understand there's a delicate balance of what she can tell us to ensure that our hopes or fears aren't swayed unjustly. As a PI, she doesn't have to play by the same rules as the police either. Some information she may not be able to turn over to them."

"Thanks, Craig. I couldn't have said it better myself." Tiff smiled. "Everything is speculation right now. I can't know for sure until I check. I just want to make sure that I explore all avenues."

"Okay." There was a tremble in her voice.

"Come on," said Craig. "I'll show you to Mallory's room."

He led the way past the kitchen and up the L-shaped stairs. After pushing open the first door to the left, Craig stepped aside to let the fairy enter.

Tiff walked the perimeter of the room while Craig watched from the doorway. The room was clean by teenage standards. Several skirts, dresses, and blouses hung over the back of a rolling chair beside a standing desk. They were likely outfits that didn't make the cut the night she snuck out. The accordion-style closet doors sat open, revealing at least five times the clothes and shoes Tiff owned. A stack of schoolbooks sat on the floor by a purple and gray backpack.

Unfortunately, bones that weren't connected to a life source lost their luster rather quickly, rendering them invisible to her senses. Attempting to locate a dead body even with a piece of 'source material' was impossible. Fairy bones, however, were an exception. Having a piece of another fairy made it possible to track them over theoretically any distance. That was part of what made gifting a crafted piece of one's self so intimate. And why Jeck's actions infuriated her so much.

Tiff unconsciously touched the pieces of Gareth's femur resting snugly in her bun. If a piece of Jeck was somewhere in the house it would stick out like a sore thumb.

She let her eyes fall out of focus and reached out with her senses. The lapis-colored walls and matching bedspread faded to a dull grey. As her awareness stretched out, she became aware of Craig behind her and Stacey's prone form downstairs. She pulled back when the mother next door bouncing newborn twins on her lap came into view. Other than her chopstick, there were no fairy bones anywhere near here. As quick as she brought it up, she let the extension of her vision fall.

Gooseflesh broke out on her arms and a dull throb rose in her head and shoulder. The room spun as her knees buckled. Tiff threw her arms out to steady herself, bringing an even sharper pain in her bad shoulder.

Craig rushed into the room and caught her before she slumped to the carpet.

"Tiff, are you okay?"

Her eyes flickered back open. Aside from her still aching shoulder, the pain faded. The tugging sensation pulling her in every direction all at once was still there. She allowed herself to stay in Craig's arms for a minute. The dizziness abated to a point she could manage.

"Thanks for the assist."

"What happened?"

"Sorry," she said, getting to her feet under her own power. "I had a dizzy spell. Probably low blood sugar." Tiff bit her lip. The silver had taken a bigger chunk out of her anchor than she'd originally thought.

"I think I'm okay now."

Tiff turned and looked back at the room as a whole. Mallory was grabbed somewhere between Julie's house and here. That meant the bracelet wasn't here. But she was here—and toothless—so she didn't have any other choices than digging through Mallory's things. If there was physical evidence to be had, she needed it more than ever.

After half an hour of digging, she came up with nothing.

"I'm sorry," she said, shaking her head. "There's nothing here. I hope I didn't get your hopes up."

Stacey rose from the couch upon hearing Tiff and Craig come down the stairs.

"Did you find anything?" she asked quietly.

"No," Craig said, moving to his ex's side. She tilted her head and let it rest on his shoulder.

"It's okay, we knew this was a long shot. Give me some time to follow up on everything else and I'll give you another call tonight."

"Thanks," he said. "I'll see you out."

Tiff gave hugs to both Stacey and Craig and then returned to her car. Once she'd settled behind the wheel, she thumbed through her phonebook and returned Jasper's call. This time when the dispatcher transferred her, he answered right away.

"What the hell happened, Tiffemory? I called all of the hospitals and couldn't find you."

"Uhm, yeah... I didn't go to the hospital. And you can just call me Tiff."

"Are you stupid? You need to get your ass to the hospital."

"That's not going to happen. Did you forget the part where I'm not exactly from here? And besides, it's already taken care of. I'm fine."

"Taken care of? You know what, I'm not sure I want to know. I presume you're not filing a police report either?"

"I called you, didn't I?"

"That's not—"

"The problem is I forced my way into a condominium because I thought my client's daughter was inside. Unfortunately, she wasn't, and I wound up getting shot."

The phone jostled on the other end, accompanied by a muffled swear from the officer. "So, you're calling to tell me that you were shot in the process of committing a home invasion."

"If you're being technical, I'd say that's accurate. But it was an extenuating circumstance. That's a thing, right?"

There was a loud sigh from the other end of the phone.

"Look, Tiff, I believe in what you've been doing. And I don't mean to sound like an asshole here, but I don't know how you think I can help you. Especially if you constantly skirt the law. You should have called 911 and reported this last night."

"I was sort of running for my life at the time."

"Yeah, I don't believe that for a second. You had enough time to call me and leave a voicemail."

"Okay, that's a fair point," the fairy said. "Could you just hear me out for a moment?"

Jasper sighed.

"Alright. Go ahead."

"I don't know whether you've heard, but Mallory Sanderson has been kidnapped again. She was who I went to find last night."

There was a brief pause and Jasper's voice took on a softer tone.

"Yeah, I heard. Next time you probably want to lead with the damsel in distress angle."

"Noted. Sorry, I'm used to working alone."

"I already know the who and the why. What I don't know is *where* they're holding her. As I was saying, I thought I found where she was being held. But once I let myself in, I didn't find Mallory. Someone was lying in wait with a gun."

Tiff made a point of leaving out the details of the silver bullet. The fewer people aware of her weakness, the better.

"Ok. But you still haven't gotten to the point where I can do something to help. Do you have any evidence? Granted, the chain of custody is beyond broken on this one, but there's potentially a life at stake."

"No. Unless a metaphysical connection to the victim by way of Tooth Fairy powers is admissible in court." Tiff glanced at the passenger seat where her purse rested. Charles' wallet was inside along with the fake ID. "I take that back. I do have some, but you probably won't like it."

Jasper let out another sigh.

"I'm going to take a wild guess and say it's a piece of stolen property."

Tiff smiled.

"Remember back at the waffle house when I mentioned how perceptive you were?" She continued, ignoring Jasper's grumbles. "Let me fill you in on a few more things.

"Two days ago, another case brought me to the airport in pursuit of another missing person case. A drug-addicted mother ran off with her child to avoid a custody battle. During that investigation, I ran into an old face—Charles Weston, the local restaurant mogul. If you recall, he was there the night of Mallory's first disappearance.

"Following him led me to another young girl who'd been kidnapped. After incapacitating him, I snatched his wallet and got the girl out of there. Now, flash forward to last night.

Who do you think I found lying in wait in the same building where I found Mallory six months ago?”

Tiff waited a moment for a response.

“Are you still there, Jasper?”

“Yeah. I’m just... digesting.”

“Oh.”

Jasper let out less of a sigh and more of a drawn-out nasal exhalation.

“I didn't know who Weston was, but I find it interesting that he’s out and walking around. I would have expected him to be in jail or prison by now. I can do some digging into that.”

“How about The Zephyr Arms?”

“What about it?”

“Can’t you investigate the condo unit too? He shot me inside the building. It’s illegal to discharge a firearm within city limits, right?”

“Technically you were shot after gaining illegal entry into a private residence. I can make some inquiries but as far as I’m aware, we didn't receive any reports of gunshots or a disturbance last night. I’m not sure if I’d have probable cause for a search if I went to investigate. Even if everything you’re saying is true—and I’m not saying I don't believe you—there isn't enough evidence to get a warrant. If I were to go and knock on the door, all he’d have to do is deny everything and we’re back at square one.”

Tiff thought back to the criminal justice classes she’d ‘attended’.

“What about exigent circumstances? What’s to stop me from calling back and requesting a welfare check on my aging neighbor that I haven’t seen in several days?”

“Sure. If you don't mind adding ‘filing a false police report’ on top of B&E and theft.”

“That’s the spirit.”

“Alright. I’ll see what I can do about having someone look into it while I research Weston’s criminal record.”

"Thanks, Jasper."

"You know, Tiff. Things were less complicated when you called me Officer Cooper."

As she scratched another item off the list, she felt better about her prospects. After flipping back a few pages of her notebook she found the address for Express Dry Cleaners and threw the car into gear.

The lights inside Express Dry Cleaners were still off when she arrived. However, the shop front faced west, and the morning sun gave her an unrestricted view inside. All of the registers were dark and nothing stirred. Tiff brought the chopstick to bear and slipped inside. A chime in the back rang as soon as she entered the building.

"Which one of you dumbasses forgot to lock the door behind you?" said a quiet voice.

Plastic garment bags full of customer's clean laundry swayed as someone pushed between the racks of the garment line machine. A man in black jeans and a dark gray tee with unrecognizable anime characters stepped out. Tiff placed him as someone in his late teens trying hard to create a persona of someone older. He had greasy, black hair slicked back except for a thick lock that fell into his face. Scraggly hairs you'd be hard-pressed to call a chin strap beard lined his chubby face.

"I'm sorry to have to do this," he said, putting a forced smile over the annoyance on his face. "But we're not open yet. I'm afraid someone didn't lock up behind them this morning." Nobody was visible behind him, but he shot a dagger-like gaze behind him. "You'll have to come back in about twenty minutes."

They stared at each other for a long moment, neither one budging. Tiff looked through him, her senses locking onto his skeletal structure without the need to physically scan him up and down. She had no intention of exerting her power over him; she had a feeling she'd need every bit of it to find Jeck, much less take him on. But it was better to be safe than sorry. Especially with what happened last night.

"You look like a Brandon."

"Yeah," he said, cocking his head sideways. "Why? Who's asking?"

Tiff walked up to the counter and held out Dawn's fake ID. He kept his eyes facing forward, studying her face instead of looking down.

"As I said, we're not open yet. And store policy doesn't require showing an ID before picking up or dropping off garments."

"Oh, it's not my ID. It's one of yours."

Brandon patted his back pocket with one hand and took the ID in his other. There was a spark of recognition in his eyes he did a terrible job at hiding.

"I think you're mistaken. This isn't mine."

"Maybe take another look. I think you're familiar with the picture and the individual responsible for forging the license."

"What are you, a police officer or something?" he said with a snort. Brandon flicked his wrist, sending the ID spiraling down onto the countertop. "I'm sorry, but I can't help you. I'm just a straight-A student who's taking time off from school to help my aging parents run their family business.

"And if you get any ideas about pulling my fingerprints off that card or some bullshit, you should know there are cameras all over." He pointed a finger at one black dome in the ceiling and then another. "They both have good angles of you handing me that thing. I don't know what you think you have, but unless it's a warrant, I'm going to have to ask you to leave."

Tiff chuckled.

"Don't worry Allip, I'm not a cop." She took another step forward, leaned over the counter, and glanced up toward the camera. "Do they record audio too? I'm curious as to whether or not my threat will be recorded."

Brandon broke out in a throaty chuckle as he looked down at the five-foot-tall, one-hundred-pound fairy.

"I very much doubt you could back up any threats you're capable of making."

"Are you sure about that? I presume you've had glimpses of what Jeck's capable of with two arms. I don't think you want to see what I can pull off with only one."

"Jeck? I don't know anyone by that name."

Tiff watched the ways his eyes moved. They barely moved when she said his name. He was telling the truth. But that didn't mean he didn't know him by another name.

"I think you do. He's about my size and is every bit inhuman as I am. I'd be willing to bet he threatened you and maybe even broke one of your bones without so much as laying a finger on you."

She knew her gamble had paid off when Brandon flinched.

"Oh..." Brandon said, rubbing his upper left arm. He dropped his arm by his side and tried to stand a little taller.

"I can see the fear in your eyes, Brandon. I assume he came in and made a polite offer to do some work for him. You tried to decline and that's when..." She reached her pointer finger out, causing Brandon to falter back a step. "He broke your arm. After he fixed it and made you the offer again, you realized you were stuck."

He flipped the hair out of his face and licked his lips. "Okay. Let's say theoretically that's exactly what happened. And that I believe you're just like whatever he is... What is it that you want?"

"In the grand scheme of things, I want the same thing you want—to get Jeck out of the way. I'll believe you when you tell me you have no idea where I can find him. But it would be a lot easier if you told me what you do know rather than going through this whole song and dance again. While I may enjoy threatening people, I don't share Jeck's enthusiasm for breaking bones."

Brandon gulped. "I'd gladly tell you where he was, but you're right. I don't know."

"We went over that already. Tell me what you *do* know. When did you get into bed with him?"

"About two weeks ago. I've gotten a couple of hefty paychecks for not much work."

Two weeks lined up with the attack Joshua suffered. Tiff nodded toward the fake ID on the counter. "That's what he has you working on? Fake IDs?"

Brandon picked it up and handed it back. "Yeah. Someone shows up periodically and drops off a bag of shirts using a code name. In the bag is a USB drive containing instructions for the desired physical characteristics. Height, weight, eye color, that sort of thing. Once I finish the IDs, I leave them in the shirt pockets. Then they go out the door as any other piece of clean laundry would."

"Do you know what they're being used for?"

He shook his head. "I know better than to ask those kinds of questions. Life's expensive and it's easy money. Besides, I don't want to know."

"Human trafficking."

"Shit. I just said that I didn't want to know." Brandon hung his head slightly. "It doesn't matter though. I know what will happen to me if I refuse."

Tiffemory balled her fingers into a tight fist. "Doesn't matter? These are somebody's friends, sisters, sons..."

"What choice do I have?"

"You knew something was off. You could have at least tried," she said through gritted teeth. After a moment, she relaxed. She had to acknowledge that Brandon was in a tough spot. She, and even Joshua, would recover quickly from a fracture. The kid wouldn't. Though, he'd have plenty of time to wallow in shame and guilt.

"You have a choice now. How many have you made?"

He shrugged his shoulders. "Half a dozen. Maybe a few more."

"Who's the client?"

"I don't know. A different person drops off the specs each time. The number attached to the customer profile doesn't even exist."

"I'm talking about the identities you created. Who were they?"

"I don't know. Random people. Like I mentioned before, the pictures came with corresponding vital information, but he left the names and addresses to my imagination."

"Okay. What about the people in the images? Boys, girls?"

"Some of each. Mostly young girls, though." He waved his finger in the air as he remembered something. "Wait. There was an old dude, too. I didn't fabricate anything for his driver's license."

"What do you mean?"

"The thumb drive always comes with specific instructions. Pictures and so on. The old guy came along with an existing ID. They wanted me to duplicate it and change the information on it. They wanted the name to stay the same. I was only to adjust the height and weight."

Tiff fumbled with her good arm to pull the well-creased paper out of her purse. "Is this him?"

"Maybe?" Brandon squinted at the printed photo. "I wouldn't say it's an exact match. He had a horseshoe mustache and the face may have been a little chubbier. But I'd say it's close enough to pass."

"Do you remember the name? Or could you print me off another copy?"

"No," he said, shaking his head. "After making the ID I destroy both the originals and all the backups. The same goes for the others. That was part of the deal. I don't like keeping any evidence lying around anyway."

"Dammit." Tiff drummed her fingers against her leg as she thought. "Do you have any way of getting in touch with these people?"

Brandon shook his head. "No. They don't show up on any kind of schedule. And it's always somebody different every time."

"Were you given anything else to hold onto? A keychain or a pendant? Maybe a money clip made of bone?"

"Bone? No. Nothing has changed hands other than cash, the ID cards, and the jump drives."

Before Tiff could think of any other questions to ask, her phone rang. The display showed Hazel's name and number.

Tiffemory pointed a finger at him. "I'm not done with you yet." She took a few steps toward the door and answered the call.

"Good timing, my leads are starting to run dry. Please tell me you've got something for me."

"I don't know whether it's good news, but I found something out. The condo unit you had me checking into was purchased recently by a Thomas Post."

"One second, Hazel." Tiff's shoulder ached when she pinned the phone between her ear and the opposite shoulder. She fished the notebook from her purse and pulled the top of the pen off with her teeth. "Thomas Post, you said?"

"That's it. That's the name," said Brandon.

Tiff scribbled the name down and took a step back toward the counter. "Can you hang on again, Hazel?" Juggling the phone, notebook, and a pen in one hand, she somehow managed to hit the mute button without accidentally hanging up.

"What did you say?"

"That name. I recognize it. Thomas Post was the name on the old man's license."

"You're sure?"

"Absolutely. I remember laughing because his initials were TP."

After staring for a moment, she wandered back to the pseudo-privacy that was the corner near the front door. She hit the mute button again. "Sorry about that. Could you find anything else out about him?"

"Some. He's a sixty-some-year-old vet. And by that, I don't mean veteran. He founded the Post Animal Hospital in Atlanta. Though it looks like he sold the practice a few years ago. Aside from some old speeding tickets, he doesn't have a criminal record. I don't know if it helps you but he's single. I couldn't find any marriage licenses on file."

"Did you come across any pictures of him?"

"Yeah, let me forward it to you. Just one second... Did you get it?"

Tiff tapped at the cellphone. In the process, she hung up on the woman. Knowing she'd call back, she fumbled with the phone until she could get the messages pulled up. A picture of an older man in a lab coat filled the screen. Without any frame of reference, it was difficult to judge his height. But the gray-haired man with a long mustache did seem to be a match for the security still Jasper had printed.

Hazel called back and Tiff answered again.

"Sorry. I think that's the man I'm looking for. Can you use my credentials to get his home address from the DMV?"

"I sure can. I'll send it via text once I get it."

"That's perfect. Thanks, Hazel. You're a life-saver."

"It's my pleasure. Promise me you'll fill me in on all the details when you wrap this up. And Tiff? Be careful."

"I will," she said with a smile.

She ended the call and dropped the notebook back into her purse. When she looked up a blonde-haired woman waited outside the front door holding a plastic bag stuffed with shirts. Tiff looked back to the counter and pointed.

Brandon turned his back and yelled to the back of the shop. "Marcus, it's 9:05 what are you doing? Get the registers set up."

Tiff waited patiently out of the way while the shop opened for business. The rest of the lights in the place came on. Another young man, presumably Marcus, came hustling to the front and placed black tills into the registers. Brandon himself came out from behind the counter and turned on the neon 'open' sign.

The woman came inside and complained about the delays. Marcus counted out half a dozen white and cornflower blue dress shirts from her bag. After giving her a receipt, he disappeared into the back and the woman went on her way.

The fairy looked over her shoulder as she approached the counter again. "That wasn't one of your specialty customers, was it?"

"No. I'm usually not up here at the registers. They always ask for me personally."

Tiff held her phone out. "Is that the man?"

Brandon took it in his hands and nodded vigorously. "Yeah, that's him." Her phone rang again, and he handed it back quickly.

Before she checked the display, she said. "Do you ever feel like every time you're in the middle of something important, your phone rings?" She slipped him a business card. "Call me before you start on any new projects."

"I get the feeling things won't end well for me if I don't follow through with his requests."

"He's my problem. When I'm done with him, you won't have to worry anymore."

The phone went silent for a moment and then began to ring anew. Tiff hurried out of the dry cleaners and answered while walking to her car.

"I need you to come down to the station," Jasper said. His tone was one of all business.

"Did you find something out about Weston?"

"Yeah. He's dead. You didn't tell me I'd be sending an officer into a crime scene."

Tiff stopped in the middle of the parking lot. A horn blared and she stepped back quickly to avoid being run over by a passing car. "What are you talking about?"

"I sent someone to do a wellness check as you asked. They found the body of Charles Weston in the back room. I need to know what the hell's going on. Pronto."

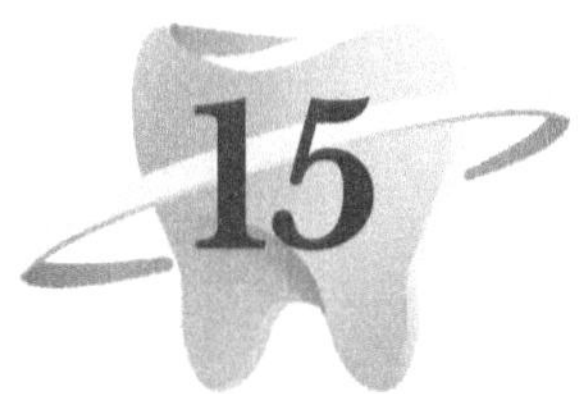

15

The lobby of the police station was relatively quiet. Tiffemory sweated as she approached the front desk. Before she could ask for Officer Cooper by name, his voice called out from behind her. She turned and found him rising from a chair beside the door. Somehow, she walked right past him.

Jasper was in full uniform this time and his lips were pulled together tight, betraying no emotion. His eyes flicked across her face while he reached for the handcuff pouch on his belt. He let his hand fall back to his side when his gaze settled upon her bandage and sling.

"Follow me," he said. His voice softened slightly and then he stepped past her.

Tiff fell into place behind him and wound her way through the building. Their destination was an empty room with a circular table with four chairs. It wasn't a formal interrogation room, but she had a feeling it was about to become one.

He shut the door and remained standing after she took a seat.

"I was worried that you'd slap a pair of cuffs on me the minute I walked in."

"Honestly, the thought crossed my mind. Hell, I still may, depending on how this conversation goes. But I suppose we both know they wouldn't hold you for long.

"Let me start by saying that I'm not officially on either of these investigations. However, nothing is preventing me from turning you over to the individuals who are if I suspect you're involved."

"Is there any harm in telling me what happened, even if you think I'm a suspect?"

"You're kidding, right? Let's start with you walking me through your version of what happened."

"Can I start from the beginning?"

Jasper crossed his arms. "I think all good stories do."

Tiff gave Jasper a recap of everything that happened in the past two days. The policeman listened closely while she detailed the events at the airport and what she learned at the abandoned motel. She followed this up with the information she gained from Julie and then ended with her fleeing the Zephyr Arms with a souvenir in her shoulder. Again, she left out the details of the silver bullet, her impromptu medical treatment, and what little she'd learned at the dry cleaners. There was no point getting Cary or Brandon wrapped up in things.

"You should have contacted the authorities when you involved yourself back at Hartsfield-Jackson."

"Nobody knew Dawn was missing at that point. As you noticed, my methods aren't exactly explainable."

"Yeah. And it's becoming more and more obvious they're quasi-legal at best."

"Still, I promise we're still on the same side." She said with a big smile. "If I wasn't, would I have marched into the police department after all this?"

He said nothing and let his eyes roam over her face.

"Did officers find the .22 round that narrowly missed my skull and lodged in the door frame of the bedroom? Because that's the point at which I ran for my life. I'm oblivious to whatever happened to Weston after that."

Jasper sighed. "Everyone in the precinct is talking about this one. Chances are that it will be leaked to the press sooner or later, so I suppose there's no harm." He took a deep breath, licked his lips, and then lowered himself into the chair opposite her. "Weston was found dead from a gunshot wound to the head. It's presumed to be self-inflicted—"

"Suicide?" The chopsticks in her hair slipped loose as she shook her head. "That doesn't make sense," she said as she put her hair up again.

"You didn't let me finish. That's not all…" Jasper's eyes went out of focus and he covered his mouth with his hand. "He… Uh… His body…"

Tiff raised an eyebrow. "What is it?"

"Weston was little more than a lump on the floor. The medical examiner said his bones were surprisingly absent."

Her stomach twisted. "What?"

"I guess that's not entirely accurate. His skull seemed to be in place. The coroner has yet to move the body and do a complete investigation, but there were no incisions they could find. Other than the obvious gunshot wound, there wasn't enough blood to have pulled off something like that."

Jasper finally raised his head from the center of the table and met Tiff's eyes.

"Is… Are you capable of doing that? Removing someone's spine without a trace?"

She broke eye contact, her voice coming out a whisper. "It would require significant time and effort, but yes, theoretically."

"Then this is the rogue fairy you mentioned? What did you say his name was? Jack?"

"Jeck."

"Putting aside the *how* for the time being… What purpose would this serve?"

Tiffemory shook her head. "I'm not sure. I don't think this kind of thing has ever happened before."

"A display of power, maybe? Thank God I haven't seen the body, but I have to imagine a boneless corpse would convey one hell of a message."

"Yeah, but a message to who? They're on the same team. Granted, Weston was a hostage due to his medical issues."

"How about retribution for Weston's failure to kill you?"

"Perhaps. There's another possibility. I threatened Charles on each of our run-ins." Tiff held two fingers up in the air. "The airport was strike two. I can't say that I planned on following through. Maybe Jeck did it for me to mock me."

"If the message is for you, wouldn't killing him be enough? What's the point of going through with the de-boning?"

"As much as I'd prefer your grisly message theory, I fear there's a different reason. He's likely using them to make weapons."

"Weapons? Are you referring to how Vikings added animal bones to molten iron for crafting swords and shields?"

"Vikings?" Tiff stared blankly.

"Yeah," Jasper said, enthusiastic that a tidbit of useless knowledge had suddenly become helpful. "They believed doing so would transfer the spirits of the slain animals into their weapons. Subsequently, those energies would imbue their blades with mystic power. But in reality, the carbon from the bones bonded with the iron to make a crude form of steel."

"If I haven't read about it, I'm not familiar with any history outside of a year ago."

"Oh, right."

"Traditional fairy weaponry is made of bone."

"I don't think I like where this is going," said Jasper as the wheels in his head turned. "If I understand this correctly...

He could do the same thing you showed me the other night at the diner."

"Turn a seemingly innocent walking staff that would slip past any metal detector into whatever sort of weapon he wished? Yeah." The officer glanced up at the chopsticks embedded in the fairy's blonde hair. "I presume those aren't large enough to fashion into a sword."

She shook her head. "A club or a hunting knife at most."

"Why don't you carry something bigger?"

Tiff frowned. "I never had the feeling I'd need one."

Jasper shook slightly as a shiver traveled down his spine. "He can't do something... worse with all of those bones, can he? Like, create some kind of golem from them? Please tell me that he's not capable of raising a skeleton army."

She shifted uncomfortably in her seat and then shook her head. "Unless he kept them on leashes, no. It's not possible to achieve that level of manipulation without direct contact." Just then a thought occurred to her. "But... He might be consuming them to replenish his reserves."

"Come again?"

"Crafting something from bone isn't a quick process. It must be extracted slowly—if you care about the donor, at least. It's also exhausting. Matter cannot be created or destroyed. If he's removing bone mass from his body, it needs to be replenished in some manner. Thanks to the information I received from Mallory's friend, I know he made her a bracelet. It's how he tracked her."

"So, he's putting bugs his kidnapped victims so he can reclaim them in the future. That makes any of your rescues temporary at best."

Tiff's mouth fell open as she came to the same conclusion Jasper had.

"Damn. I need to find Dawn."

"You think she's in trouble? I'm not an expert in all things tooth fairy, but I would have thought you'd have noticed something like that."

"Bad timing. When I found Dawn, I'd just tracked down another client's son. For a lack of better words, I was wrapped up in a gratitude high and in a rush to get Dawn out of there." She sighed. "If I had scanned all of her, instead of just the leg that had a cast on it, I wouldn't have noticed it."

"No time to dwell on the past," Jasper said, getting to his feet. "We need to go now then."

"We?"

"If there's a girl's in trouble, I'm coming along."

"No offense, but it's probably better that I go alone. I can handle this myself."

"Even with your bum shoulder?" The door handle gave a quiet creak as he turned it halfway.

Tiff chewed on her top lip, drawing a bit of blood from the already raw skin. She looked up at the officer without moving from the table. "I asked you to check into Charles before he wound up dead. Did you learn anything helpful?"

Jasper opened the door and held it for her. "Yes. I'll tell you on the way."

Tiff let out a low growl. It was abundantly clear he wasn't letting her out of his sight. If she wanted to keep Dawn safe and get to the bottom of things, she had no choice but to let him tag along.

"Alright. As long as you understand what you're getting yourself into."

He smiled. "I'll drive."

Officer Cooper held the office door open for the fairy and led her out the back door to his waiting cruiser.

"Alright. Where's the address I'm going to?" he said once they'd both buckled in.

"Hang on," Tiff said, pulling out her phone. "It's in this stupid thing somewhere."

It took her a few minutes, but when she finally scrolled back through her navigation history, she handed the phone over. Jasper copied the address into the onboard computer system.

"Are you going to hold up to your end of the bargain and tell me what you learned about Weston?" Tiff asked after they left the parking lot.

"Aside from his infamous DUI, the man's record is clean. The problem is that it shouldn't be. He was detained the night of Mallory's original kidnapping and there were multiple witnesses to it.

"The main suspect who disappeared—Jeck—took full responsibility for everything. The third man had priors that ended him back in prison. Even if Weston turned state's evidence, I would expect to see something on him."

"Okay. What's your take?"

"I don't know. It's feasible that Weston's an informant and that's why there are no records. From a low-level standpoint, turning someone into an informant is handled at the officer's discretion. After picking up a teenager on possession, I could theoretically offer to forgo a charge if he offers up his dealer.

"However, something as serious as kidnapping is a different story. That would require a police asset with specific training in handling CI's. That would also be something that's logged in the system. Unfortunately, I haven't gone through any of that training, and very few officers have access to that database."

"I don't want to offend you by suggesting blatant police corruption... But have any of the officers with said training returned unexpectedly from a medical or disability leave?"

Jasper turned his head and locked eyes with her.

"Did I get too close to home?" she asked.

"You could say that..."

Tiff could see the wheels turning in his head.

"Before you sling any accusations around the office, let me fill you in. This fits Jeck's MO to a tee. Weston was in a similar boat. The crash resulting from his DUI was near-fatal. Jeck patched him up and virtually eliminated his recovery time. He's also been keeping his bone cancer at bay.

"I'm sure you understand how easy it would be to blackmail an individual you could cripple in a heartbeat. Jeck likely started asking for small favors before things spiraled completely out of control."

"Huh. I had no idea you could heal people too."

"That's not entirely accurate. Given the knowledge, broken bones are a piece of cake to mend. Slipped discs are a little trickier but can be nudged back into place without much of a problem. Brain damage, internal bleeding, severed spinal cords: there's still no coming back from injuries like that."

"So, why become a private eye instead of a doctor or an X-ray tech? Wouldn't that be the best way to use your powers to help others?"

"How did law enforcement handle Jeck spontaneously disappearing from his cell? And what do you think would happen within the medical community when miracles started happening every day? I have a feeling that kind of attention wouldn't be healthy for me."

"For not knowing much about human history, you've got us pegged. How many people know you're a fairy, anyway?"

"I don't know. Half a dozen, maybe. I'm sure there are a few others who have suspicions that I'm not quite right."

"Oh." Jasper's eyebrows rose. "I guess I should feel flattered you decided to trust me."

"Not to make you feel less special, but I felt the potential good outweighed the harm. Even if you tell your superiors about me, they'll think you're crazy. I have to imagine that would be a career-limiting move."

"Gee. Thanks..." Jasper drove in silence for a few miles.

"Would it be the worst thing in the world if more people knew?"

"From the little bit of your history I've studied, I haven't found a great track record when it comes to tolerance of anyone different."

Jasper rubbed his goatee for a moment. "Okay, that's fair. So, what exactly brought you here?"

She gazed out the window into the distance. "I couldn't stay in Fae."

"If there's not that many of you here, I'd have to presume there wasn't a mass exodus due to a natural disaster. Were you thrown out? Or are you just running from something?"

Tiff reached up for the comforting touch of the chopsticks lodged in her golden hair. "I... I lost my husband and little girl. There were too many reminders of them to stay."

"Oh." He licked his lips and dipped his head. "I'm sorry, I didn't know."

Tiff gave a weak nod.

They drove in silence the rest of the way to the U-shaped drive of Dawn's boyfriend's house. As Tiff shifted in her seat to exit the vehicle, Jasper gently placed his hand on her injured shoulder. She turned to face him.

"Before we go up, can I ask you something else?"

"Sure. What do you want to know?"

"Are you... Are tooth fairies invulnerable?"

"No." Tiff raised her left arm, sling and all. "Exhibit A."

"I guess what I want to know is whether normal bullets—that is, non-silver ones—are effective against them?"

The hairs on her neck stood up. "You pieced together the silver thing, huh?"

Jasper gave a sly smile.

"Yes. We bleed just the same as anyone else."

"So why are you hesitant to let me provide backup?"

Tiff licked her lips and let go of the door handle.

"I acknowledge the training and experience you have as a police officer. But I have no way of knowing what I'm walking into. No offense, but your experience amounts to nothing when dealing with Outsiders. I can't directly affect Jeck or his partner with my powers and vice versa. You're open season."

She shifted to face him. "Look at it this way. Wouldn't it be reckless if you brought a civilian along while responding to a dangerous call?"

Jasper opened his mouth to speak but closed it and then nodded.

"I can appreciate that. But you're forgetting that I'm not a civilian. As you said, you're not from here, but I am. And it's my job to protect the populace from these types of situations. Well, maybe not *these* situations, but the sentiment still stands."

The officer got out of the car and then leaned back inside to address the fairy one last time before shutting the door.

"You're injured and outnumbered. You need all the help you can get."

Jasper and Tiff stood shoulder to shoulder on the porch of the two-story Tudor. After ringing the bell, he leaned toward her and whispered.

"Dawn isn't one of the people who know you're a fairy, is she? I wouldn't want to let it slip."

"No. The poor girl didn't ask too many questions on account of being sedated."

"So how do we approach this?"

"Just follow my lead."

Jasper snorted, stood up tall, and straightened out his uniform. A moment later the door swung open to reveal Mitchell's massive profile.

"Honey, the girls are here," he said before turning and realizing the people on the stoop weren't who he'd been expecting. "Sorry officer, I thought you were someone..." As he shifted his gaze to the fairy his lined face broke into a jubilant smile.

"Tiff, it's good to see you again." The man stepped forward, prepared to wrap his bear-like arms around her. When he noticed the sling, he adjusted mid-stride and clasped both hands around her right forearm instead.

She smiled and lingered in the man's grasp. Tiff's eyelids fluttered as she savored the residual warmth of the man's gratitude. It wasn't anywhere close to replenishing all she'd lost the other night, but it was a start. Jasper was right. She needed all the help she could get.

"Where are my manners?" He reached out and shook Jasper's hand. "I'm Mitchell, Kevin's father. Please come in."

As Jasper and Tiff stepped into the entryway, a woman in a white ruffled top, a white skirt, and a sun hat with a black bow hurried down the stairs. She came to an abrupt stop on the landing when she saw Jasper.

"Ow," she mumbled as the suitcase she'd been pulling slammed into her ankle. "Is everything alright?"

"This is my wife, Anna," Mitchell said, sweeping his hand toward the stairs.

Anna descended the remaining steps more carefully. She looked like a toddler next to her six-foot-five husband.

"Everything's fine," Tiff said. "I wanted to check up on Dawn and ask her a few more questions. If that's alright, of course."

Mitchell turned toward Jasper. "I'm not her legal guardian, but it's okay with me. I offered to bring her to the station so she could file a report, but she hasn't been very receptive to the suggestion. I think they're—"

Two quick horn blasts came from outside. Anna excused herself and opened the front door to reveal a limousine parked beside Jasper's squad car.

The woman turned back to her husband. "We still have plenty of time before our flight. If you want me to stick around..."

"It's fine," Mitchell said. He stepped forward and gave his wife a hug and a kiss. "Enjoy yourselves and be careful."

Anna hurried outside with a suitcase in tow. Brief screams of glee could be heard through the door before the limo pulled away again.

"Sorry about that. My wife and her friends take an all-girl trip every June. Last year was Napa Valley and this one is Vegas. I think Kevin and Dawn are in the basement if you'd like to follow me."

Mitchell led them through the kitchen to a door near the back of the house. He ducked beneath a beam at the bottom of the stairwell where the hardwood floors transitioned to plush carpet. The basement was a veritable man-cave. A billiard table sat near a pine bar on the left side of the room. A projector mounted from the ceiling shone onto a framed wall on the opposite end.

Kevin, a boy with blonde hair spiked in the front, craned his neck from the black leather sectional.

"Dad? Why are the cops here?"

"Would it be alright if we talked with Dawn for a few minutes?" Tiff asked.

Dawn, who'd been resting her head in Kevin's lap, sat up at the sound of the fairy's voice. She squeezed her boyfriend's hand and started to get to her feet.

Tiff walked around to the front of the sofa. "You don't have to get up. I came by to check up on things. How are you doing?"

"I'm okay. I'm still hazy on some of the details from the other night. And I don't think I'm ready to talk about it yet. But Kevin and his family are taking good care of me. I don't know what I'd do without them."

Tiff glanced back to see Mitchell beaming.

Kevin straightened up. "But why is there a police officer here? What's going on?"

Dawn glared at her boyfriend and opened her mouth to say something.

"I don't want to alarm you," Tiff said. "But we believe the individuals who took you may have implanted a tracker beneath your skin. There's no reason to think you're in any immediate harm... But if my suspicion is correct, we should remove it as soon as possible."

"What?" Mitchell said. "Like an RFID transmitter vets implant in dogs? Those things can't be cheap. What kind of sickos are we dealing with?"

Jasper nodded. "Ones who have no place within Atlanta."

"Is there a specific medical facility we should go to have her checked out?"

"That won't be necessary," Tiff said without hesitation. "I've removed others and it's a quick and easy process. Dawn won't feel a thing and there will be little to no blood. Trust me."

Kevin got to his feet. "Why didn't you mention this the other night?"

"It's okay," Dawn said, pulling her boyfriend back down to the couch. "I trust Tiff. Let's just get this over with. What do I need to do?"

Tiffemory turned to the girl's surrogate father. "Could I trouble you for an ice pack, some paper towels, and a plastic cup?"

"Yeah. Of course. Whatever you need." Mitchell ducked behind the bar and came back a moment later with the items.

Jasper shifted in place near the stairs. "Do you need me to do anything?"

"No. Why don't the two of you wait upstairs so we can have some privacy. I'll need Dawn to slip off her shirt." Tiff chewed on her lip and hoped it was in her torso. The poor thing had been through enough already.

Mitchell looked to Dawn, who nodded her agreement and then headed upstairs with the police officer.

"Is it okay if Kevin stays?" the young girl asked.

"Of course." Tiff looked to the bar in the corner of the room before deciding it would be easiest if she went to them. "Please scoot to the edge of the couch. Kevin, you can pull the ottoman over and sit across from us."

When the door clicked shut at the top of the stairs, Dawn shifted on the couch and pulled her shirt over her head.

Tiff climbed onto the couch, straddling Dawn from behind. She closed her eyes and extended her senses into her fingertips. While it would limit the range, it would also minimize the energy expenditure. If a piece of Jeck's bone was here, it should be easy to find.

The fairy placed her right hand on Dawn's lower back. She let the fingers of her right-hand trace back and forth across the teenager's warm, pale skin. The lumbar spine was clear, as was the thoracic and the floating ribs. She continued her sweep upward. When they passed over the base of her neck dozens of tiny, painless pinpricks tickled her fingertips. She let her hand rest there.

"Did you find anything?" Dawn asked when Tiff's hand lingered.

"Yes. But don't worry, it's shallow. I'll remove it."

Tiff's fingers probed millimeters at a time, letting the prickling sensation act as a braille-like guide until she could visualize the outline of the offending bone tissue. The first rib, situated between the cervical and thoracic vertebrae, had a section of bone that most certainly didn't belong.

Kevin leaned over Dawn's shoulder. "Are you going to give her lidocaine or something?"

"It's not necessary. The ice is to numb the skin before I extract it. Don't worry, all you'll feel is cold and perhaps a tiny amount of tugging."

Tiff pressed the blue, rectangular ice pack to Dawn's neck. The girl jumped at the cold, and then slowly settled back down where she'd been. Of course, the ice pack was only for show. But the placebo effect worked wonders.

Kevin held both of Dawn's hands in his and smiled. "I'm right here. If it hurts, squeeze my hands. "

"Okay, Honey," Tiff said. "Try to sit still."

The fairy centered her pointer finger, middle finger, and thumb firmly over Dawn's spine while doing her best to hold the ice pack at the same time. She closed her eyes and directed her power. Dawn's skin bulged slightly outward as

Jeck's bone pulled free from her own. With another exertion of energy, a thread of bone the width of a hair pressed its way outward, pushing through muscle, tissue, and finally skin. It gathered in the void between Tiff's extended fingers and started to wind itself together into a solid mass once again. In two minutes, she held a piece of white bone half as thick as a pair of dice.

She dropped the bone into the plastic cup, wadded up a piece of paper toweling on top of it, and then slid out from behind the girl. With only one good arm, it wasn't as graceful as she intended.

"See, all done."

"Really? That's it?" Dawn touched the back of her neck and brought her hand before her eyes. "There's no blood."

"I told you that you could trust me."

Kevin's eyes followed Tiff as she stuffed the cup into her purse and zipped it closed.

So, what now?" he asked. "Will that lead you to the people who did this to her? Are you going to make sure that they don't do this ever again?"

"That's the idea."

Dawn put on her shirt, stood up, and hugged Tiffemory. The fairy groaned under the squeeze as a lance of pain shot through her shoulder and reverberated down her arm. The young girl pulled away at once.

"Oh my God, I'm sorry. What happened to your arm?"

Tiff looked down and frowned.

"I'm in the middle of another case and things aren't going so swell. But if I'm lucky this tracker might be what I need to close it."

"I'm sorry."

"I'll be alright. More importantly, how are you doing, Dawn?"

"Okay, I guess." She looked down at the floor for a moment and then shook her head. "Not really... I've been having nightmares."

Tiff nodded. "You need to see a therapist. It will help to talk about it. If money is a concern, there are state-supported programs that won't cost much. I know people who can point you in the right direction."

Dawn looked up again and embraced Tiff again, though more carefully this time.

"Okay," the girl whispered. "Thank you."

The fairy wrapped her good arm around Dawn's waist and squeezed. "If you need anything, let me know." She retrieved a business card from her purse and pressed it into her hand. "I mean it."

"Okay. I will."

"I hate to cut this visit short, but I have some other matters to attend to. Take care of her," Tiff said to Kevin before heading back up to the main floor.

Jasper stood near the top of the stairs with Mitchell pacing behind him. He stopped when he saw the door open.

"Dawn's fine. I didn't have any issues getting the tracker out. If you want to go down and see her, we can see ourselves out." Tiff started to backtrack her way through the house and then turned around to face Mitchell again. "Thank you for everything you've done for her. When we talked before, she mentioned how complicated her home life was."

"Are you kidding? I should be the one thanking you. She's a sweet girl and we've considered her to be part of the family almost as long as we've known her. Even if she and Kevin break up, she'll always be welcome here."

Jasper shook Mitchell's hand and said, "Thank you."

Tiffemory climbed back into the passenger seat of Jasper's squad car and pulled the cup from her purse. The piece of bone rattled around inside as she gave it a gentle shake. A drop of blood hit the back of her hand and she realized she was chewing at her lip again. She pressed her tongue to the raw spot and held it there until it stopped.

Nothing would have given her greater pleasure than destroying the rotten piece of her nemesis. It turned her stomach to think about what had to come next. The bone wasn't given freely and trying to track Jeck with it would only further drain her anchor. She had to swallow it.

"Are you okay?" Jasper asked, handing her a tissue.

"Yeah," she said, wiping off the back of her hand. "I split my lip the other night, that's all."

"So that's it?" he said, pointing to the cup.

"Yeah. Jeck—or the other fairy—grafted a piece of themself near Dawn's spine. If I'd done a more thorough job examining her in the airport, I could have put an end to things two nights ago."

"Oh, come on, you can't fault yourself for that. An officer's primary duty is to safeguard life. I'd say you succeeded in that." Jasper licked his lips. "Can you track them using that like you would a child's tooth?"

"One of them. Though I have to presume they're sticking together."

Jasper started the cruiser and rested his hands on the steering wheel.

"Okay... So how does this work?"

Tiff knew telling him the truth would only lead to him insisting on coming along but nothing had changed. As much as she didn't want to face Jeck alone, she couldn't ensure anybody else's protection. Much in the way that she couldn't protect her husband and daughter.

She tilted her head down and to the right before blinking away the tear in her eye.

"I need some time to prepare. First, I need to do some legwork to get a rough trail. After that, I'll swallow this piece of bone. If I'm close enough, it will lead me directly to the source. The good news is that the bones of Outsiders are different. They aren't metabolized in the same manner and are much more accurate at greater ranges."

"And the bad news?"

"It will take me at least twelve hours to fixate my energies on that source."

Jasper let his hands fall back into his lap. "I guess that's it then. I'll drop you off back at your car..." Tiff's phone chirped and buzzed in her purse, momentarily interrupting the officer. "And then we can pick things up in the morning.'"

Sounds good."

Tiff checked her phone, angling it so only she could see the screen. The text was from Hazel. She got Thomas Post's address and information on his criminal history—which was non-existent. From Hazel's prior warnings Tiff knew the data might be a few months old, but it was the best she'd get on such short notice.

The hint of a smile touching her face didn't go unnoticed by Jasper. He glanced in her direction.

"What is it? Something relevant to the case?"

"No," she said with a shake of her head. "Just a work friend giving me an update on her blind date from last night. She was excited to finally meet her mystery man." There was a pang of guilt about lying to Jasper, even if it was for his protection.

Jasper chuckled and pulled to a stop behind her yellow Toyota in the visitor's lot of the precinct. He turned in his seat to face her. "I expect you to call when you know something."

"I'm going to stop for something to eat and then I'll get started. I'll let you know what I find but it might be pretty late."

"That's okay, I'll be up."

Tiff closed the door to the squad car and settled into the driver's seat of her vehicle. After acquiring directions to the address Hazel provided, she pulled out of the lot. The navigation system complained as she headed in the opposite direction. For starters, she wanted to ensure the officer wasn't following her. And one thing she told Jasper was the truth. Her growling stomach needed tending.

Sublime Doughnuts was her favorite go-to in the city. The shop operated twenty-four hours a day out of a strip mall near Georgia Tech. She swung by and grabbed her usual: a caramel apple fritter and an Oreo burger. Contrary to the name, the latter wasn't a burger in the traditional sense. Sublime's creation consisted of gelato with cookie bits slathered between two doughnuts. And it was the best thing Tiff had ever tasted.

She took her sweets and sat down on one of the two couches in the shop. In record time she devoured the burger. The second doughnut wasn't far behind. Before finishing it, she pulled the plastic cup out of her purse. Tiffemory pressed the fragment of Jeck's bone into the last bite of the caramel apple fritter.

"Let's get this over with."

She closed her eyes and swallowed the remnant of the donut.

17

Halfway to the veterinarian's house Tiffemory reached down and closed the navigation app on her phone. The connection to the other fairy was strong enough to find her way without it. She twisted and turned her way through winding suburban streets until she arrived before a large, granite fountain beside a gatehouse.

Through the little booth's tinted window, she could barely make out a small monitor. When nobody slid the window open, she accelerated and passed through the open fence of the gated community.

Just like in Weston's neighborhood, her little Toyota was out of place among the Bentleys and Jaguars parked in driveways and open garages. Thomas Post's house was a three-story all-brick monster with a perfectly manicured yard. As Tiff took in the sights of the mansion, her car wandered up onto the curb. She slammed on the brakes and came within inches of plowing into a mailbox fashioned to look like a miniature version of the house behind it.

"I told myself I'd stop driving around while doing this," she said aloud. Tiff backed the car off the curb and parked it directly in front of the rut in the parkway.

Tiff grabbed her purse, opened the passenger door, and planted one foot on the concrete. Before she got out, she brought Hazel's text back up on the screen of her phone. She tapped the arrow indicator near the top of the screen to forward the message and selected Jasper's contact card. The text cursor blinked, waiting for the message to be sent.

She turned her attention back to the house and closed her eyes. Ideally, she'd be able to differentiate a man from a woman based on the structure of the pelvic bone. Unfortunately, the foreign piece of bone slowly moving through her digestive tract made that discernment impossible. What she could tell was that there were three occupants inside the house. The two hazy outlines on the lowest floor were humans. A single fairy resided above them, shining like a beacon.

One of the unknown occupants had to be Mallory. The other was probably another kidnapped boy or girl. It was hard to celebrate the fact that she'd only have to take on a single opponent. Even if she was outnumbered, she wanted to be rid of them immediately. Tiff crossed her fingers and hoped it was Jeck and then slipped her phone back into her purse. There was no reason to notify Jasper. So long as she could catch the fairy off-guard, she wouldn't need any help.

Tiff surveyed the scene again. The house was massive. Two roman columns beside the double front door held up a balcony on the second floor. The fairy was in a seated position on the ground floor, perhaps in a study or something. The other two figures were near each other in the basement. Her shoulder was stiff as she pulled her arm out of the sling. She left it on the driver's seat and headed up to the house—she couldn't portray any weaknesses.

She circled the house looking for a way in. Five window wells were spaced around the sides of the house. Unfortunately, she couldn't make out anything through the soaped over windows. Even if she could safely lower herself down, getting any wounded or drugged captives back up with her injured shoulder was a bad idea. She needed to find another way. Tiff moved to the back of the house again. The

174

door off the deck was the furthest entry point away from the person in the study. It was her best bet.

Although the glass sliding door exposed her, her adversary hadn't shown any sign of movement. Tiff carefully gave the door a slight tug. To her surprise, it slid open on a well-oiled track. She stopped and focused her senses again. None of the three individuals inside appeared to have noticed her.

Something in her head warned her that this was a trap. Her mind flashed back to images of Charles Weston's boneless corpse. With that much material who knew what Jeck could accomplish. Her head spun and dizziness set in, forcing her to focus back to her mundane senses. She'd come too far to walk away.

Tiff took a deep breath, removed one of the syringes loaded with silver nitrate from its protective sheath, and stepped inside the house. The kitchen smelled of fresh vanilla and lemons. Tiff slipped her shoes off and left them beside a handful of empty dog bowls. Her bare feet moved without a hint of sound on the dark hardwood floor.

The pull to the other fairy was overwhelming. She stuck close to the walls and followed the pull that seemed to thrum with life through the very air. The entryway was clear. She moved to the foot of the stairs and peered around the corner. Beyond a sitting area with numerous paintings of Paris lay a pair of French doors leading into the room where the rogue fairy resided.

With no option for an unseen approach, Tiff hid the syringe behind her forearm and stepped into the room lined by built-in bookshelves. The man inside wasn't Jeck but *was* a dead ringer for the man in Jasper's printout. He sat on a leather armchair angled in the corner and looked down at the book in his lap. There was an air of high society behind him. He wore a white dress shirt beneath a sweater and a pair of expensive-looking loafers.

While he bore an uncanny resemblance to Hazel's picture of the veterinarian, something was off. He had the same cheekbones and broad nose but no mustache or jowls. The facial lines of a man his age were absent too. There were no signs of aging at all. Either Thomas Post recently had a facelift or the man in front of her was his son.

"I've been waiting for you," the man said without looking up. "What took you so long?"

Tiff pushed through the cracked door and set foot in the room. Old fashioned sconces shed soft light over the floor to ceiling bookshelves.

"Thomas Post, I presume?"

The man balanced his book—a copy of Mein Kampf—on the arm of the chair.

"Or a semblance of him, anyway," he said with a toothy smile.

Tiff took another look around the room before directing her attention back to the man. He hadn't attacked her. Maybe she could find a peaceful resolution.

"I don't know who you are or whether you know what you're wrapped up in, but you're working with some bad people. If Mallory's here, I'm taking her. If not, I strongly suggest you tell me where she is."

The man let out a hearty laugh. "What are you going to do? Spew a veiled threat about how this is my second strike? Or maybe you plan to hit me with that lame arm of yours."

Tiffemory narrowed her eyes. "What did you say?" She wracked her brain, trying to place his voice or his face. Something told her that he knew her. And she should have known him.

"Come now... You honestly have no idea who I am?"

"Not Thomas Post?"

It took him a considerable amount of time to get to his feet. But when he finally did, the fairy broke into an even larger grin.

"Thomas Post is in the chest freezer in the garage. I guess it's his face that's confusing."

He lifted his head and looked down his nose at her. Suddenly his face shifted a bit to the left. More accurately the *bones* beneath his face shifted to the left.

Tiff's eyes bulged. There'd never been a second fairy. The fairy in front of her rearranged his facial structure to resemble the veterinarian. His voice was a slightly different pitch, but that too could be changed with bones putting pressure on his vocal cords.

"Jeck…"

"As you can see, I'm a new man, Tiff."

Jeck put his arms out and did a little spin. She noticed the hideously deformed right hand Jasper mentioned the other night. It reminded her of the burls on the massive oak trees back in Fae.

"I should thank you for sending me away. You wouldn't believe the things I learned from the Exiles while I was there."

"Exiles?" she muttered under her breath. The only exiles she was aware of were myths. They were her culture's equivalent of the boogeymen used for the sole purpose of keeping little children in line. Tiff pulled her lips together tightly and took a step closer.

"I've made more acquaintances here too. They're beneath the likes of our kind, but powerful in their own right. Since you can't possibly understand the things now set in motion, I'm inclined to give you a second chance."

Tiff took another few steps, getting within striking distance.

"And what happens to Mallory if I agree to whatever your demented terms are?"

"She'll be free to go. I can go down to the basement now and fetch her."

"That's all I needed to know."

Tiff lashed out with the syringe, catching him square in the chest. The tip of the needle caught him square in the chest... and snapped. Silver nitrate dribbled out of the now useless plastic tube. It tumbled from her hand and she retreated a step.

Jeck laughed and crushed the broken syringe under one of his loafers. The rogue fairy took a rigid step forward and wrapped his left hand around Tiff's neck before she could grab the second syringe. Her feet dangled and he lifted her a few inches off the floor. The purse strap slipped off her shoulder and fell out of her reach.

Tiff's eyes fell out of focus, looking for a weakness to exploit. Jeck glowed as if he were irradiated. Her jaw dropped. There weren't individual ribs in his chest; his torso was one solid carapace. Aside from a few strategically placed gaps and joints to allow for articulation, his entire body was an exoskeleton of interlocking plates. Removing Weston's bones had nothing to do with making weapons.

"Impressive, isn't it?"

"Disgusting is more like it," she spat. Tiff beat against his forearm and struggled to break from his grasp.

"One more thing," Jeck said, touching the back of his malformed hand to Tiff's belly. "You have something that belongs to me. And I'm going to need it back."

He clenched his fist and Tiff let out a bloodcurdling scream. Seconds later a corkscrew-shaped piece of bone burrowed its way out through her skin. Once free, it melded back into Jeck's hand.

Tiff's golden hair fell around her shoulders as she plucked the chopsticks from her bun. As she drew it down the pieces of bone morphed together into a six-inch-long, serrated dagger. It slashed along Jeck's forearm, tearing chunks of his skin as it went. He howled in pain although there was all superficial damage thanks to the newly grafted bone.

Jeck raised his fist. The large bony outcropping around his knuckles receded. A piece of tattered cloth fell, still hanging on. Tiff saw the glint of silver only for a moment before it slammed into her cheek. She groaned, blood dripping from her mouth. He hit her again. And again.

He shuffled forward, slamming her back against the wall. Books tumbled to the floor as she kicked. Stitches in her shoulder popped as she deflected another strike with her left arm. Instead of attempting to hit her again, he sandwiched her arm between his fist and the wall.

Sprawling purple bruises broke out on her skin and Tiffemory screamed. Her entire body vibrated and felt like it was being pulled apart by a team of wild horses. The dagger slipped from her grip, reverted to the statue of a winged fairy in mid-air, and tumbled across the blood-spattered floor.

"Before you're violently removed from this world, I'd like to hear what your plan was," he said, removing the silver from her skin for a moment. "Banish me again and wait for me to come back ad nauseum?"

She took a giant heaving breath, blood dripping down her shoulder and gut. Jeck was a veritable walking tank. Her multi-tool was on the floor and her husband's bone somewhere in the corner of the room. It was hopeless.

Then, Tiff thought about all the other children who may have been polluted with Jeck's bones. And poor Mallory was tied up in the basement. She was their only hope. There had to be a way to stop him.

A lightbulb went on in her head and the medical journal she'd been reading the night of Mallory's disappearance came to mind. She laughed aloud, drawing a renewal of the sharp pain in her gut. She summoned all the power she had.

"Let's see you come back from this," she said panting.

Tiff raised her knee into Jeck's groin. Before it even connected, bone mass from her femur, pelvis, and spine surged downward at her command. An enormous bone spike tore through the skin of her knee. It raced upward, tearing through Jeck's unprotected organs and piercing his heart. He lost his grip on Tiff and stumbled backward.

She slumped down the wall and let out a rasping chuckle. Medical science was right. Sometimes the fastest way to a man's heart was through his groin.

"You'll regret this..." he said, collapsing to the floor. "I promise."

The two-foot-long spear protruding from her knee glistened with blood. It retracted slower than it should have and took its sweet time to disseminate back to the places it belonged. Every inch of her itched, like bugs scuttling beneath her skin. Her body twitched as the universe pushed and pulled at her, taking advantage of her failing anchor.

Somehow her shaking fingers managed to check for a pulse on Jeck's neck. He was gone. She pushed her way to her feet. Even having beaten Jeck, it was all for naught if she didn't manage to get Mallory out alive. He had partners here, she was sure of it. Him being gone didn't necessarily change anything.

Tiff crawled to her purse and hit send on the text she'd drafted to Jasper. Even with everything the officer knew, she didn't know how she'd explain any of this. There was no way to keep this quiet. Word would eventually get out about the anomalous bones encompassing the body in the library—not to mention the grapefruit-sized hole in the man's groin.

A loud thump echoed from somewhere in the basement startled her. She leaned forward and fell to her knees as the thumping grew louder and closer. The walls shook as a door slammed into the opposite side of the wall. A moment later there was a second slam and a breeze swept through the house.

It took her almost a minute to get the bone statue and to her feet. Blood streaked across the floor as she stumbled into the front room. Through the open front door, she caught the backside of a man bolting down the street. She breathed a heavy sigh of relief. At this point, a toddler could kick her ass. Tiff lurched to the side and knocked over an end table. She clung to the wall, fighting against the forces attempting to expunge her. Time wasn't on her side but once she made it to the girl, she'd be okay.

The railing along the stairway to the basement bore the brunt of her weight as she descended. She stumbled on the last step and fell into the room. Three chest-high kennels lined the western wall of the unfinished space. Mallory cowered in the cage farthest from the stairs. Her brown hair was chopped to shoulder length, about half as long as it had been when Tiff last saw her. Instead of the brown sweater from Julie's picture, she wore a plain white dress shirt with a school sweater several sizes too big—Jeck's cruel attempt to put her in the same outfit as when she'd been kidnapped the first time around.

Tiff pulled herself to her feet and limped closer to the cage while clutching the hole in her stomach with the hand of her wounded arm.

"Don't hurt me!" Mallory screamed, pressing against the back wall of her prison.

"Mallory, it's me. It's Tiff. I'm going to take you back to your dad."

"Get away from me... Whatever the hell you are." Mallory's eyes darted to the area past the fairy and then drifted back.

Tiff turned her head and noticed the television mounted to the wall. It showed the library upstairs, where Jeck's body lay in a growing puddle of blood. The poor girl saw everything, as had whatever lackey who turned tail and ran.

The fairy turned to face the girl again, but Mallory wouldn't even meet her eyes.

"I..."

The color drained from Tiff's cheeks and a frigid cold gripped her body. The room lurched sideways and she crashed into the metal cage, driving the air from her lungs. All she could do was hold onto the cage and the fairy statue for dear life. That became increasingly difficult as tremors gripped her body.

Her fingers fumbled with Gareth's statue and managed to pinch the tip of one wing into a slender pick. Still keeping a death grip on the cage, she slipped it into the cheap padlock. No amount of shimmying the makeshift tool made it pop open.

Tiff nestled the statue beneath her armpit and stuck her hand through the gaps in the cage. "Take my hand..."

Mallory screamed and cowered in fear.

Tiff lost her grip on the wire mesh. The purse slipped off her shoulder and hit the cement floor. She screamed as forces threatened to pull apart her body like a dingy trapped in an ocean squall.

***

Mallory covered her eyes, protecting them from the blinding flash. When the after images in her vision settled, she crawled forward slowly and checked the dark corners of the room. She craned her neck and stared at the monitor. That bastard was dead, and the house was quiet. The teenager scurried to the front of the kennel and grabbed Tiff's purse.

Inside was the multi-tool that... that *thing* had with her the last time she rescued her from Jeck. Mallory grabbed it and unfolded the blade. She set it aside and grabbed the phone. There was a sigh of relief when it came to life without a password prompt.

Heavy footsteps clambered down the stairs. Mallory took a step back, hiding the knife behind her back. That creep was gone but she'd sooner die than be taken by someone else.

"Hello?" a voice called. Moments later, a uniformed officer came around the corner.

"Help," she cried... "Get me out of here!"

Tiff's world went black. In the span of a heartbeat, the bleak basement was long gone. As were the empty cages lining the walls and the terrified girl that was worth giving up everything for. Tiff pressed her hand tight to the bleeding gash in her gut. She reached around her, but the token of her husband's love was gone.

Her screams went unanswered as she drifted through the nothingness between realities. Despite there being no wind or any sense of motion, her stomach did jumping jacks like she was on an airplane capable only of traveling in parabolic arcs. She fought to keep down the bile that scrambled up her esophagus with each dip.

After what felt like an eternity, her stomach settled as the powers that be finally spat her back out where she belonged. Darkness gave way to sunbeams streaming through the trees. Her throbbing heartbeat was replaced with the sweet chattering of birds. Then there was that awful feeling of falling and she landed face first in the mud.

Pain reverberated up her left arm and into her shoulder. She gasped and took a deep breath. The scent of pine and wildflowers tickled her nose. It felt... off—somehow, she'd grown used to Atlanta's exhaust-choked air.

She didn't have the strength to move. It felt like she'd been through a fire. Every bit of her burned and stung but her only thoughts were of Mallory. Hopefully, Jasper got to her in time.

Tiffemory's story is not finished. It picks up immediately with EXILES, the 2nd book in the Osseous series. I hope you enjoyed and don't forget to leave a review on Amazon and/or Goodreads!

Acknowledgements

The dedication covers most of the individuals I wanted to convey my thanks to, but I'd be doing a disservice without providing any elaboration. My wife has been more than patient with me over the past few years as I sat in the corner of the basement every night typing away like a madman (as opposed to playing video games and shouting into a headset like a madman).

After my longest running beta reader disappeared, Annie picked up the slack and devoured the entire backlog of the series. She's continued to be patient every time I fire off an email questioning the merit of certain chapters or plot points.

Last, but certainly not least, I owe a great deal of gratitude to my cousin, Josh. I've barely an eye for graphic design, which he excels at. We worked together to attempt a cover design for this book. Unfortunately, I led him astray because I haven't the foggiest when it comes to what urban fantasy covers look like. I ultimately went with a professional. However, Josh continued to lend his eye when I tried my hand at ad graphics, bookmark design, and the like. He also delivered one bad-ass trailer.

I couldn't have succeeded in this task without his guidance and kind words.

About the Author

Michael grew up avidly playing Dungeons & Dragons with other, like-minded nerds. These activities fostered a vivid imagination that he still remembers fondly.

Since becoming an "adult" with "responsibilities", the days of 10-hour binge sessions are long gone. Writing has now become the official outlet to keep his mind entertained. He loves urban fantasy and is excited to share his reinterpretation of old myths with a broader audience that a few individuals huddled around a table.

Michael lives with his wife and two children in the suburbs of Chicago. During the day he works full-time in IT. Once the screaming of children has subsided in the evening, he retreats to read, write, and/or absorb himself in video games.

A Tooth Fairy's Promise is his debut novel.

You can follow Michael via these outlets:
Facebook: @DerelictBooks
Instagram: @MJAAuthor

Stay up to date by joining his newsletter: